HIDE OR DIE

The Secret Pack Trilogy

Hide or Die
Fight or Fly
Truth or Lie

The Packverse Trilogy

All for Knot: Book One
All for Knot: Book Two
Knot for Sale

The Knot Playing Fair Trilogy

Knot Playing Fair: Book One
Knot Playing Fair: Book Two
Knot Your Victim

HIDE OR DIE

EMBER BLAZE

Hide or Die (Secret Pack, #1)

Copyright 2021 by OtherLove Publishing, LLC

All rights reserved. Printed in the United States of America. No part of this book may be used or reproduced in any manner whatsoever without written permission except in the case of brief quotations embedded in critical articles or reviews.

This book is a work of fiction. Names, characters, businesses, organizations, places, events and incidents either are the product of the author's imagination or are used fictitiously. Any resemblance to actual persons, living or dead, events, or locales is entirely coincidental.

ISBN: 978-1-955073-18-9 (paperback)

For information, contact the publisher at www.otherlovepublishing.com/contact/

Cover art by Ember

First Edition: September 2021

Author's Note

Secret Pack is a human omegaverse trilogy where the main character doesn't have to pick one person in the end. It features protective alphas and the omegas who love them, but no shifters. The series is intended for a mature audience.

Table of Contents

ONE

Leona

CONSIDERING I'D risked my life to be here, I wasn't enjoying this party at all. The ballroom inside the Hotel Epoque in Bucharest had been decorated to resemble nothing so much as an explosion at a wedding cake factory. Around me, the other VIPs who would be attending the upcoming Transatlantic Summit on Alphomic Policy were mingling politely, drinks in hand.

Like everyone else present, I was dressed to the nines. My forest green velvet evening dress had been chosen to highlight my fiery red hair. Makeup thick enough to hide my nervous pallor presented a facade of approachable feminine beauty to the outside world. Jewelry hovering just on the right side of gaudy dripped from my earlobes, throat and wrists, as I cradled the martini I was pretending to nurse and smiled pleasantly at everyone who greeted me.

Inside, I was waiting for the metaphorical ground to crumble beneath my four-inch designer stilettos. It was a feeling I'd grown used to over the years, since it was almost always present, hovering in the background of my sham of a life. Tonight, however, I had more cause than usual to worry.

Kameron Patel hurried toward me through the crowd, trying valiantly not to *look* like he was hurrying. Lithe and graceful in his tailored tuxedo, he slipped through gaps in the throng like a shadow, ignoring the appreciative looks he garnered from most of the female guests and more than a few of the male ones as he passed.

I smiled blandly as he reached my side and cupped his hand beneath my elbow — the small point of contact easing a fraction of the tension from my shoulders. Placing my untouched martini on the tray of a passing waiter, I allowed myself to be herded subtly toward the dance floor.

"He's just arrived," Kam murmured in my ear, his light, Indian-accented voice too low to be heard by anyone else above the rising hum of conversation.

I gave a tiny nod to let him know I'd understood, and settled into his arms. We smoothly inserted ourselves into the glittering whirl of other couples waltzing around the floor to the accompaniment of a string quartet playing Tchaikovsky.

"They say he has the sharpest senses of any beta alive," Kam said, still too low for any other ears but mine. "Leona, I'm scared for you. This was too risky."

Anyone watching us would see nothing more than a short, curvy, redheaded beta woman dancing with a black-haired, olive-skinned beta man of average height and slender build, but with an unusually beautiful face.

They'd be wrong on both counts.

Since the Purge began more than a century ago, omegas like us had three choices. Submit to slavery, undergo sterilization and become second-class citizens, or hide in plain sight as betas and take our chances in a world that despised us. Thanks to rich beta parents who'd cared more for their child's freedom than their own safety, I'd had the luxury of the third option. The omega in my arms—who now played the role of my trusted colleague—had, in succession, experienced all three of those things during the course of his thirty-five years.

That we'd achieved as much as we had was almost unheard of in a world run by betas. Thanks to a combination of ambition and the subtle evolutionary advantages conveyed by my omega status, I'd enjoyed a meteoric rise through the diplomatic corps in the United Federation of North America. Black market heat blockers and pheromone suppressors had so far prevented anyone from detecting my ruse. Of course, that toxic cocktail also practically ensured that I'd succumb to one form of cancer or another within the next couple of decades, if I didn't somehow manage to get off them soon.

Kameron, meanwhile, had escaped his fate thanks to help from the secret underground that acted as a support system for alphas and omegas lucky enough to find a contact there. Inserted into a new life stolen from a random dead beta, he was now my diplomatic attaché. Both of us had found a place in the UFNA's new liberal administration, shaping policy that might one day help our kind escape from beneath the bootheel of the global beta supremacy movement.

I squeezed Kam's hand, trying to convey reassurance as we whirled effortlessly around the dance floor. "It'll be fine," I murmured. "We knew the bastard wouldn't let something as important as this summit happen without showing up in person to try and thwart it."

"He's a monster," Kam whispered, barely audible even at such close range.

"Yes," I agreed. "He is."

———◆———

Kostya Nikolayev was a familiar figure in the news media. Tall and broad-shouldered, his very presence seemed to draw all the air from a room. Even from across the dance floor, the effect was far more overpowering in person than it was when experienced through the filter of a television screen—unsurprising, since one did not rise to the top echelons of an influential worldwide para-governmental organization by being a wallflower.

As the newly installed head of the Euro-Soviet branch of the Committee on Alphomic Suppression, Nikolayev had a vested interest in ensuring that the upcoming summit didn't strip any power from his organization. For decades, most of the world's major nations had allowed the Committee to take the lead in defining policy related to the subjugation and eradication of alphas and omegas.

Apparently, our very existence perverted the natural order of things, or so the argument went. We flew in the face of beta religious teachings about the roles of men and women in family and childbearing, with our polyamorous mate-bonds and 'unnatural' decoupling of the concepts of sex and gender.

Never mind the fact that alphas and omegas had been around every bit as long as betas. Female alphas had been siring pups on male omega carriers—and vice versa—since before humanity started banging rocks together. For us, gender didn't matter—only reproductive plumbing. Alphas sired pups. Omegas carried them. Mated packs formed on the basis of emotional compatibility, regardless of the number or gender of the pack members involved.

The perennial hostility of those in power toward beta homosexual liaisons was multiplied a hundredfold when it came to alphomic social structure. Betas feared alphas as being generally stronger and more dominant. Meanwhile, they secretly desired omegas, seeing us as both inherently submissive and inherently corrupting.

Alphas were mindless brutes that would take over if given the chance, immediately hurtling humanity back to the Stone Age. Omegas were weak slaves to their own sexual natures, who would drag good, upstanding betas into their sinful ways like sirens luring sailors to their doom. Those were the old slurs... the old lies. For millennia, the push-pull of hatred and reconciliation had rolled over human civilization in never-ending cycles. For a few generations peace would reign, until eventually some group needed a convenient scapegoat and turned on alphas and omegas to provide it.

The latest round of persecution—and the rise of the Committee—had started some eighty years ago in response to increased global poverty, climate change, and the mechanization of jobs at the turn of the century. *'Alphas are stealing all the good jobs!'* came the rallying cry. *'Look at all these good-for-nothing omegas squeezing out pups! They take resources and give nothing back!'* And so began the calls for ever-more repressive laws and ever-more stringent penalties, until it became a full-blown witch-hunt of anyone with a knot or a mating gland.

People whose parents would have loudly proclaimed against the evils of slavery began clamoring for controlled breeding programs to produce chemically castrated alphas for use as unpaid labor. Laws requiring omegas living outside of the breeding plantations to be permanently sterilized became commonplace. In most parts of the world, being an unregistered alpha or omega was now a capital offense.

At the heart of it all stood the Committee. And at the heart of the Committee stood Kostya Nikolayev—a beta renowned for his cruelty. He was said to have personally tortured and executed his adolescent female omega sibling when she refused to report to the slave camps. According to those who'd confirmed the death, the body had been barely recognizable after he'd finished with her.

The fact that he was from an impure beta bloodline—one that had historically interbred with alphas and omegas—should have been an obstacle in his rise to power. His reputation for ruthlessness ensured that it hadn't been.

And now he was here, in the same room as me. The same room as Kam. A man who was said to be able to sniff out any omega within twenty paces, regardless of pheromone suppressors.

It was probably an exaggeration.

Almost certainly.

I hoped.

"He looks like a Bond villain," Kam muttered, *sotto voce*.

I elbowed him as discreetly as I could manage. It would be more accurate to say that Nikolayev was feared by those in political power than to say that he was liked—but there was no reason to tempt fate by saying things like that in public.

Not that Kam's observation was entirely inaccurate. Broad shoulders... iron-gray hair streaked with silver... thick, neatly trimmed salt-and-pepper beard... two-piece charcoal suit at odds with the sea of black tuxedos around him... he looked like a man who considered this entire soirée beneath him. It was clear that he'd come here for the sole purpose of ensuring no ground was lost in the political battle to subjugate my people and wipe out dissenters—not to waltz or hobnob with political dignitaries.

A hand touched my shoulder, and it was all I could do not to jump.

"Madam Ambassador," said a pleasant male voice.

I turned to see a vaguely familiar face and immediately started flipping through my mental Rolodex to attach a name.

"Secretary Fouchet," I replied, forcing warmth into my voice. "What a pleasure to see you again. Heavens, how long has it been?"

The departmental official from Luxembourg smiled, obviously pleased that I'd remembered him. "Oh, a good year at least," he said. "It was that meeting of the western regional authority in Paris, wasn't it?"

"Yes, I believe you're right," I said, slipping into my role with the ease of long practice, despite the presence of the mass murderer in the room.

"You're looking particularly lovely tonight. May I request the honor of a dance?"

Fouchet asked, extending a well-manicured hand to me, palm up.

"Of course," I told him. "It would be my pleasure."

I took his hand and flashed Kam a brief look, meeting his unhappy brown gaze before heading off to play the part of the socially competent diplomat.

Fouchet was a pleasant enough dance partner—prone to the subconscious beta attraction to an omega-in-hiding, but too polite and self-possessed to step outside the bounds of professionalism. He also waltzed well enough that I was in no danger of mashed toes—at least, not until the moment I caught sight of Nikolayev and another official I didn't recognize looming over Kameron. Kam's absolutely straight spine spoke of base terror barely contained.

I nearly stumbled over my own feet, and Fouchet steadied me as we came to an ungainly halt in the middle of the dance floor.

"Forgive me," I managed, in response to Fouchet's solicitous murmur of concern. "I must have slipped on something. I'm not usually such a clumsy dance partner." The words sounded far away to my own ears, and I was barely aware of the details as I extricated myself with enough grace for it not to seem out of place or unusual.

After thanking him for the dance, I walked in something of a daze toward the potential train wreck in progress across the ballroom. *If he can sniff out hidden omegas, he'll also be able to smell fear*, I told myself. *You're a respected UFNA ambassador. Act like it.*

Shoulders squared, chin up, I approached the little cluster of three, aware that others in the immediate vicinity were also turning to look. Kam formed the uneasy vertex of an acute triangle as the other two stood side by side, facing him.

"Ah," he said, in the tones of someone who *wasn't* two seconds away from losing his shit. "Madam Ambassador. I was just telling Chairman Nikolayev and his associate that you would be pleased to discuss the proposed policy changes with them once the summit begins tomorrow."

"Ambassador McCready." The Chairman cut across any opening gambit I might have made, foregoing the proper *'Madam'* honorific as he addressed me. "Is it true that Prime Minister Fairbanks intends to negotiate new restrictions on the current alphomic extradition treaty between the United Federation of North America and the Committee's international tribunal?"

His deep voice seemed to press down on my shoulders, accented with the sharp vowels and growling consonants of his native Russia. I had to physically fight not to bow beneath its weight.

"All of the proposed points of debate are included in the documents outlining the summit agenda, Chairman," I replied pleasantly, no hint of my struggle coming through. "And as Mr. Patel has indicated, I will be happy to discuss them with you once the summit is underway."

Gray eyes a few shades lighter than his utilitarian charcoal suit jacket pinned me, as though trying to peel back the layers of my skull and see inside. I wanted to grab Kam by the hand and flee. I wanted to fall to my knees on the marble floor and roll my head to the side, baring my throat in submission. I wanted to scan the room for our security detail, just to make sure they were there.

That last impulse was the hardest to quell, and while it might not prove quite as disastrous as either of the other two options, it was still an unacceptable show of weakness. I had no doubt Kam was fighting the same urges, and the knowledge that he was strong enough to resist them gave me that same strength. I raised an eyebrow, projecting unconcern.

The nameless sycophant at Nikolayev's side shifted restlessly. "The Committee will not countenance interference in the great work by an upstart administration barely six months into its tenure."

"Then we will have much to discuss, it appears," I told him with false brightness. "I look forward to it. But for now, I'm afraid I must return to a discussion with Secretary Fouchet. It was a pleasure to speak with you."

I gave them both a polished smile and gestured for Kam to precede me toward a larger knot of dignitaries near the buffet table, having glimpsed Fouchet among them.

"Good evening, gentlemen," Kam said politely, before turning and forging a path through the ever-shifting crowd. I followed, feeling the back of my neck prickle almost painfully under Nikolayev's gaze.

TWO

Leona

NOW THAT Nikolayev couldn't see me doing it, I cast my gaze around until I found Chief Beckett standing unobtrusively against the wall, one hand pressing against his earpiece as he spoke into a discreet communications mic pinned to his lapel. His pale blue eyes locked with mine, and he gave me a curt, reassuring nod. A tall, dark-skinned alpha stood nearby, arms crossed. His black tuxedo jacket barely managed to contain the bulging muscle of his massive biceps as he watched over the scene impassively.

The other two members of our security team would be nearby as well, keeping an eye on events. My spine relaxed incrementally, the animal terror of the past couple of minutes fading to manageable levels.

"God in heaven," Kam muttered, like someone who'd narrowly escaped being run over by a bus.

"Hush," I told him, leading him toward Fouchet and the other dignitaries as though nothing at all were wrong. The secretary looked up from his conversation and smiled.

"Luca," I greeted warmly. "I don't believe you've met my attaché, Kameron Patel…"

The rest of the evening passed like dripping molasses, until I began to think it would never be over. We managed to dodge Nikolayev successfully for most of it—omega self-protective instincts coming to the fore. When his presence was unavoidable, there were at least other people present to react to his complaints about the proposed negotiations with greater or lesser degrees of sympathy, deflecting some of that unbearable intensity away from us.

When the party began to break up around eleven p.m., I was more than happy to settle into the middle of a protective phalanx formed by Chief Beckett and our three alpha guards, with Kam at my side—sheltered from the outside world.

Beckett cleared his throat as we entered the elevator that would take us from the ballroom to our suites on the hotel's top floor.

"Madam Ambassador, I'd like to do one more sweep of both of your rooms before you retire."

I glanced at him, surprised. "Weren't they checked earlier?"

"They were," he confirmed. "I'd like to check them again."

"Very well, if you think that's best," I agreed, after only the slightest of hesitations.

Rhys Beckett was one of the most respected security experts in the business, with decades of experience under his belt. This trip was the first time he'd been assigned to us, but if he and his team of alpha underlings wanted to double-check our rooms, they probably had a good reason to do so.

Subjugated alphas had become slightly more common in security roles within the UFNA in recent years, since the expansion of an experimental military program that allowed them to access more specialized training in a carefully controlled environment. And, of course, every unit containing alphas still required oversight by a trusted beta team leader.

Beckett had volunteered to lead such a unit, whereas most betas would have resisted the assignment. Rather than trying to out-alpha the alphas under his command—a task that would have been laughable, given his mild voice, unprepossessing physical frame, and affable demeanor—he seemed almost paternal with them much of the time. I wondered what they really thought of him... these alphas who'd traded their virility for this limited form of freedom.

It was dangerous to think about the alphas, though. Even though they'd been chemically castrated, allegedly to make them more *tractable*, they presented a temptation I didn't need. I didn't even know their names, and I intended to keep it that way. Simply being trapped in an elevator with them like this was nearly overwhelming, with my upcoming heat only days away.

In addition to the dark-skinned giant, there was a sandy-haired male who was all sharp cheekbones and sinewy muscles, along with a statuesque female who moved like some kind of stalking jungle cat.

All three of them smelled *divine*… and that was a perfect example of the kind of thought I couldn't afford to indulge. Beside me, I could practically sense Kam going soft and doe-eyed. I resisted the urge to mash his foot with my stiletto heel, knowing there was no way to make the move anything other than obvious to our stoic protectors.

Deflection was needed—or perhaps distraction, in Kam's case.

"What makes you think our rooms might be compromised?" I asked Beckett. "Should we be worried?"

He gave me a thin smile. "No, I don't believe there's cause for concern. It's merely a matter of logistics. Normally I would have stationed a guard in the hallway to ensure no one entered your rooms while you were absent. However, with Nikolayev and his retinue attending the function downstairs, it seemed more prudent to have the extra manpower stationed in the ballroom—especially given the current political climate in the region."

I nodded in understanding. "Ah. Right. So the rooms weren't watched, meaning someone could have snuck in and planted a listening device while we were at the party."

"Exactly," Beckett confirmed. "Best to be sure."

The elevator dinged, opening onto the lavishly appointed fifth floor. Not all of the summit attendees were staying here, but the Fairbanks administration had spared no expense to ensure that Kam and I would not be forced to commute across Bucharest to a different hotel on the night of the pre-summit soirée. It was yet another manifestation of the unlikely career success we'd carved out, against all odds. Sometimes, I still had to pinch myself.

'Tall, Dark, and Overpowering' stepped into the hallway first, looking in both directions as though he expected assassins to leap out at us wielding AR-15s. The other two alphas fanned out behind him, and Beckett ushered Kam and me out with an economical gesture of one hand.

Kam fished our keycards out of an inner pocket and handed me mine.

Our rooms were next to each other, but didn't share an interior door. I'd noted that fact when we'd first checked in. Now, I mourned it. After facing down a man who would happily see both of us dead if he knew our secrets, I had no desire whatsoever to spend the night alone. I doubted Kam did either.

Over the years, we'd carefully cultivated the impression of a discreet but still mildly scandalous extracurricular affair. Despite the whiff of unprofessionalism, given that Kam was my attaché, it was occasionally useful to portray the picture of a *normal beta relationship* to the outside world.

It wasn't normal, and we weren't betas, but it still helped to deflect suspicion.

However, this wasn't the time or the place to be seen sneaking in and out of each other's rooms during the night. We opened our adjacent doors, sharing a glance.

Beckett's eyes flicked to his female alpha underling. "Alex, take Flynn and check Room 508. Jax and I will take 506."

So much for not knowing their names.

The no-longer-nameless *Alex* gave a brisk nod and disappeared into Kam's room with the dark-skinned alpha — Flynn. Kam tagged along behind them like a love-struck puppy, and I suppressed a sigh. Beckett and the sandy-haired alpha, Jax, entered my room. I followed, staking out a corner away from any lights or electrical outlets, where I wouldn't be in their way.

The space was light and airy, with a huge glass patio door leading onto a balcony. I hated it. Everything about it made me feel exposed and on display, from the walls painted sky-blue to the glow of city streetlights visible through the sheer curtains.

I wanted a nest and I couldn't have one, because having a nest might expose me for what I really was.

The knowledge itched at my insides. Even in my own apartment back in Montreal, it was too dangerous to do anything permanent with the decor that might scream *'omega'* to an observer. I was an ambassador. I entertained. The idea of some random beta bureaucrat stumbling across a dim, red-lit room full of pillows and furs piled on the floor didn't bear thinking about.

I could picture the screaming headlines now — *'High-Level Unregistered Omega Outed in the Most Idiotic Way Possible! News at Eleven!'*

So instead, I huddled in the corner of this horrible, open, sky-colored room and watched the familiar dance of a security team sweeping for bugs. So far, no security team assigned to me had ever found one. To be honest, I was a bit curious at this point to see what a bug actually looked like.

I crossed my arms and leaned back against the ugly blue wall, impatient to get off my feet after a night of dancing and standing around in heels. Maybe I'd hide away in the bathroom and take a hot bath with the lights off later, once the others had left.

Despite my best intentions, my eyes locked onto the blond alpha like steel filings drawn to a magnet as my thoughts drifted. That was the only reason I saw his shoulders stiffen as he pulled the cover from the electrical outlet next to the bed.

"Found one, Chief," he said, and straightened a moment later with something grasped delicately between his thumb and forefinger.

Beckett grunted acknowledgement, even as I pushed away from the wall, shocked.

"Seriously?" I asked. "Can I see?"

The alpha—*Jax*—turned toward me as I approached, palm extended so I could get a look at what was resting in it. My first thought was that it was tiny. The rectangular circuit board had a small metal cylinder attached to one corner, the top of which was made of a fine mesh, like a microphone. That made sense, since that was exactly what it was.

"Wow," I said inadequately.

Beckett looked less than pleased. "Right. That's unfortunate. Madam Ambassador, I would strongly suggest moving to a different room rather than relying on us to find every bug. There may well be multiple devices hidden in here. For now, let's see if they've found anything next door."

We did, and found Kam watching wide-eyed as two painfully attractive alphas dismantled every electronic device in his room.

"We've turned up two so far," said the one called Alex. Her voice was low and smoky, with a Quebecois accent.

"There was one in the phone handset, and one in an electrical outlet," Flynn added.

Beckett gave them a curt nod. "Well done. These two are going to have to change rooms, and we'll definitely need eyes on the hallway tonight. We'll take guard duty in shifts."

Still somewhat in shock that anyone would go to the effort and risk of breaking into our rooms and planting listening devices, I didn't protest when Beckett asked us to stay here in Kam's room with his alphas while he went down to the lobby to sort out new accommodations for us. He pocketed the three devices the others had uncovered, presumably to use as leverage in case the hotel manager balked.

"Just don't talk about anything you wouldn't want to be overheard," he said dryly.

Jax snorted in poorly veiled amusement.

Except for that single noise of dry humor, the alpha security guards were the picture of stoic professionalism after their team leader left. Kam stood awkwardly next to the TV, arms crossed, trying not to look anywhere that might get him into trouble. I crossed the room and sat in the desk chair, wishing I could toe off my heels without it coming across as too familiar. The idea of being barefoot beneath the alphas' impassive eyes twisted something deep inside me — not entirely unpleasantly.

I quashed the sensation ruthlessly.

The silence was becoming unbearable when Beckett finally returned with a harried-looking hotel employee in tow.

"I'm so terribly sorry about this, Madam Ambassador," the man said in heavily accented English. "I can only apologize on the hotel's behalf. We will, of course, make available all security camera footage from the hallways during the time in question."

"Thank you," I said coolly, rising to my aching feet. "For now, though, what we really need are new rooms. Preferably ones *without* secret listening devices installed."

The man winced. "Yes. About that..."

I raised an eyebrow.

He cleared his throat. "You must understand, with the summit..."

"They're booked solid," Beckett said.

"We do have a double available, thanks to a last-minute cancellation," the hotel employee added quickly, a hopeful tone entering his voice. "I understand it is not ideal, but there are two queen-sized beds, and the view from that side of the building is lovely..."

Beckett gave me a questioning look, since chivalry dictated that a beta woman would be the one to decide whether she wanted to share a room with a beta man who wasn't either a relative or her husband.

I had to swallow back the groan of relief that threatened to escape, burying it beneath a cool facade of indifference. "I imagine we can make it work for one night. Kameron? Are you all right with that?"

"As long as you don't snore, I'll make due," he quipped. "But you should be aware that I hog the bathroom."

The employee nodded enthusiastically, with the air of a man who knew he'd dodged a professional bullet. "Excellent. I'll have someone sent up to move your luggage right away."

I exchanged a final glance with Kam, and went to pack up my toiletries. Twenty minutes later we were installed in a different but equally awful room, designed by someone who apparently thought glass was a reasonable substitute for a wall.

Though the bathroom was quite nice, at least.

Beckett insisted on a sweep of this room as well, but it came up clean. When we were settled, he reminded us that someone would have eyes on the room throughout the night, and that the motorcade would be leaving at seven the next morning. As soon as the security team left, taking their distracting scents of musk, cypress, and sandalwood with them, I slumped onto one of the beds and flopped backward onto the mattress, toeing off my heels, my arms spread wide. Kam perched on the edge next to me.

"I'm still shaking," he said, quietly enough not to reach alpha ears in the hallway outside.

"Yeah," I agreed.

"We must be insane."

I nodded, not lifting my head. "Yeah."

Silence stretched between us, comfortable in its familiarity.

"The rooms in this place are terrible," Kam said at length.

"The worst," I concurred. "I feel like a butterfly pinned in a glass case."

"Do you think, if we're quiet…?" he began, before trailing off.

I knew exactly what he was asking. It was a risk—but this close to my heat, my judgment was apparently becoming suspect. Mostly, though, I needed a decent night's sleep before wading into battle with Nikolayev and his Committee tomorrow.

"All right," I said. "We can hang the do-not-disturb sign, and there's a swing latch on the door. We'll have to put everything back well before dawn, though."

"I know," he said. His hand closed around my thigh and squeezed lightly. "Dibs on the bathroom."

"Diva," I told him, without any real heat.

He rose and crossed to the door, opening it just enough to hang the DND notice on the doorknob outside. With that accomplished, he shut it and swung the bar-latch closed for extra security. Together, we dragged a mattress off one of the beds. Being careful not to knock anything over or otherwise make noise, we jammed it into the gap between the two bed frames, where it formed a squashed U-shape on the floor. While he went to take a shower, I pulled the woefully inadequate curtains closed across the offending wall of glass, and gathered all of the available pillows and blankets together.

When it was my turn in the bathroom, I peeled off my velvet evening gown and hung it up carefully. After removing my makeup and brushing out my waist-length red hair, I stepped into the shower, turning my face into the warm spray. I emerged some time later, blow-dried, plaited, and wearing a thigh-length silky nightgown.

In my absence, Kam had finished constructing our makeshift nest by stretching one of the blankets over the gap between the beds, weighting the edges with our suitcases to form a tent-like covering. A single lamp cast a pool of soft yellow light in the darkness of the room. With a heartfelt moan of relief, I lifted the front edge of the hanging blanket far enough that I could crawl inside and wriggle into Kam's arms inside the soft, womblike space.

THREE

Leona

WE SQUIRMED around until we were both comfortable—arms and legs tangled together, pillows jammed around us to stand in for the bodies of other nonexistent packmates. The U-shaped sag of the mattress kept us pressed close, and the blanket overhead reduced the glare from the single lamp to a soft, diffuse glow.

The smell was wrong—laundry detergent and furniture spray rather than *us*. Between my weekly dose of pheromone suppressors, and... what had been done to Kam when he was young, the nest wouldn't take on our scent no matter how long we huddled here. But aside from that, everything else was as close to being *right* as it ever got for people like us.

I burrowed my nose into the place where Kam's neck met his shoulder, taking comfort in the act of scenting him even if there was, in reality, nothing to scent. He gave a tiny shiver, and a heartbeat later, all the tension drained out of him at once. He pressed his cheek against my hair, and the breath flowed out of his lungs in a slow exhale.

"Needed this," he murmured.

Me, too, I thought—but that was another dangerous thing to think.

"Just for a few hours, though," I whispered against his skin. He nodded silently, and I pressed my lips to the skin over his mating gland in apology.

A tremor ran through his body in response, gooseflesh rising in its wake. One of my thighs was pressed between his, and I felt his vestigial omega cock twitch through the thin cotton pajama bottoms he was wearing. Despite the black market testosterone injections he took to stimulate beard growth and make building muscle easier, I knew that it wouldn't harden any further than that.

Kam and I shared every intimacy, and in safer surroundings than this, we gave each other what pleasure we could, when the desire arose. But biology limited us in a number of ways. It wasn't 'sex' in the way that betas defined sex. It wasn't 'mating' in the way that alphas and omegas experienced mating.

It was just... *us*.

Keeping the dark at bay.

Not being totally alone in the night.

"Leo," Kam said, still in a tone so quiet that not even alpha hearing would be able to hear it through the muffling blanket and the hotel room wall. "I am absolutely terrified for you. You shouldn't even be here. Not so close to..."

He trailed off, unwilling to say the word aloud in a building filled with betas, even though none of them would be able to hear. And wasn't that the perfect metaphor for what omega life had become? Here we were, huddled together in a nest that would be more than sufficient cause to have us both hauled off for physical examination and genetic testing if we were caught, yet Kam couldn't bring himself to say *'so close to your heat.'*

"I've got my meds with me," I reminded him, not for the first time. The bottle of aspirin in my suitcase contained five pills that were visually indistinguishable from all of the others—but an omega's nose could sniff them out easily enough. Four were pheromone suppressors that, taken weekly, would keep me from perfuming for up to a month. This, despite the fact that we were only slated to be here for six days before returning to Montreal. The fifth pill was my heat blocker, which I would take three days from now to head off the estrus that would otherwise be on me within the week.

Kam's arms tightened around me. "They're not meds, Leo. They're *poison.*"

A lump grew in my throat, but I swallowed it down. "They're tools, Kam. Tools with side effects, yes. But what else am I supposed to do? Drown myself in *Chanel No. 5*? Take a week's vacation every three months like clockwork? How long do you think *that* would fly before someone noticed?"

Kam made a miserable noise against my hair, and shimmied down until he was the one burying his face in the crook of my neck. "I *know*," he said, disconsolate. "But I'm still allowed to hate it, all right?"

"Yes—all right," I soothed, rubbing my fingers through the fine hair at the nape of his neck. I'd always loved his hair—so thick and black, but fine as silk beneath my touch. "I concede that you're allowed to hate it. Could we just... not talk about it right now, though?"

I didn't need Kam to remind me that the toxic cocktail of drugs I required to hide condemned me to some form of cancer in my future—it was a fear that hung over my head in my waking present, and each time I popped one of the pills that were both my salvation and my ultimate demise. And when that day arrived, any attempt to get medical treatment for that cancer would instantly out me as an omega.

I could either live now and die later, or suffer through a half-life of slavery and die anyway, eventually. I'd gone into this with my eyes wide open.

Besides, I'd ridden out one heat cycle on my own—my first one. And I *never* wanted to do that again. Suffering through that dayslong, desperately painful craving for sex and closeness when those cravings could never be fulfilled? It was a form of torture—both physical and mental.

Once upon a time, omegas had looked forward to their heats as a time for unparalleled sensual pleasure, the potential for pups, and possible bonding with one or more mates. But that was not my life.

"I'm sorry," Kam said, still holding me tight. "I didn't mean to upset you. I know you've got it under control. You're the strongest person I know."

Then you must not have looked in a mirror lately, I wanted to say. The words stuck in my throat. I couldn't get them out, and he wouldn't have wanted to hear them anyway. I took blockers to short-circuit my heats. Kam, on the other hand, would never have heats at all. And I knew with utter certainty that if he hadn't been mutilated as an adolescent, he would have cheerfully risked exposure and arrest to experience that part of an omega's life as it was meant to be experienced. He would have sought out alphas, no matter the danger... or in the absence of that option, at least a trustworthy beta male. He would have made beautiful pups one day, and whelped them in secret. He would have been the best, most loving and devoted carrier any pup could ever ask for.

"I'm the one who's sorry," I said. "Being here with you like this—it should be perfect, and I'm ruining it."

Kam let out a dissenting noise, and burrowed into me a little further. "You're not ruining it, *odama*," he said, using the ancient word for a co-omega in a mated pack. A pause, and then he added in a teasing tone, "Though it would be even nicer with some alphas to help warm the nest. Three of them, I think. That sounds about right, doesn't it?"

Dangerous, warned the little voice in my head that kept me safe. *Don't go there, even in fantasy.*

Would it really kill me not to be a repressive bitch one hundred percent of the time, though? I might be too scared to go there, but Kam wasn't. Kam still believed in a world where happy endings were possible. Did I seriously want to shoot him down when it came to his harmless daydreams, as well?

I swallowed my misgivings and reached for something, anything that wasn't fatalistic pessimism.

"I'm pretty sure we'd need a bigger nest," I managed, and was rewarded with the pleased curve of his lips against the skin of my throat.

"Oh, yes," he agreed. "We'd need a *huge* nest." A happy sigh. "Just think—all of those lovely muscles. And that female—Alex? Did you *see* the way she moved?"

I couldn't help it—an answering smile tugged at my lips. "Kam. I love you, but you're a terrible clit-slut. You do know that, right?"

He scoffed. "*Excuse you*. I am an equal opportunity slut, at least inside my fantasy world. But yes, that is one clit I'd *definitely* like to tease out of its sheath with my tongue, and ride all night long…"

I settled into the snug nest of pillows and blankets and *friend*, letting Kam narrate all of his increasingly filthy imaginings regarding the trio of alphas assigned to keep us safe in this faraway land. And if some of those fantasies made me squirm against his body a tiny bit, I put it down to my approaching heat.

Nothing more.

———◆———

By four a.m., we had the nest dismantled and everything returned to its rightful place in the room. Thanks to the happy endorphins still sloshing around in my system, I even managed to get another ninety minutes of sleep before my alarm went off.

By seven, we were settling into the black limo that would take us from Bucharest to the much smaller city of Târgovişte, nestled at the base of the Southern Carpathian Mountains. The summit would take place at an ancient monastery in the foothills. It was, in my opinion, a somewhat odd choice of venue. As far as I'd been able to determine, the place's main claim to fame was that Vlad the Impaler's father was buried in the narthex of the monastery's church. Which was… historically interesting, I supposed?

It was probably meant to be symbolic of the resurgence of the Church in Eastern Europe over the past couple of decades. Or... something. If nothing else, the architecture was apparently well regarded by people who were interested in such things—not that there was likely to be much time or spare energy for playing tourist during the summit.

The motorcade pulled out of the hotel's grand circular drive and into the bustle of the city. Kam and I were in the middle car, with Jax riding shotgun in the front seat, next to a driver I didn't know. The other two alphas, Alex and Flynn, were in the lead car, while Beckett was in the one bringing up the rear, along with some additional support staff from the Foreign Office.

I gazed through the tinted bulletproof window, idly watching the city slide by as I attempted to center myself in preparation for what promised to be a grueling few days of negotiations. Romania's capital was an attractive muddle of old and new, but it was mostly the old that dominated. Even some of the relatively new landmarks, like the massive Palace of the Parliament, had been built to evoke a sense of times past.

It took almost an hour to negotiate the morning traffic and reach the outskirts of the city. For a while, cropland dominated. Before long, however, the landscape turned into parched and dusty scrubland. Even here in Europe, the twenty-year drought had driven agriculture down into the river valleys, where reliable irrigation was simpler to engineer.

Through the front window, I could just begin to make out the Carpathians, shrouded by morning haze. Mountains always made me think of home—not Montreal, but rather, the tiny town in Colorado where I'd been born. Not that the place was really *home* these days—my beta parents lived far away from there, having taken on new identities and moved to the Caribbean, where the Committee held less sway.

They'd had to uproot their lives to protect themselves because *I* existed. In fact, I'd insisted on it, once my career in the diplomatic corps started to take off. They'd given me a chance at a respectable beta life—but the moment my cover was blown, theirs would have been blown, too. They had aided and abetted an unregistered omega throwback, rather than handing me over to the authorities and washing their hands of me as soon as they'd discovered my true sex.

Now, whenever my house of cards inevitably came tumbling down, an investigation would find that both of my parents had been tragically killed in a car crash six years ago. Mr. and Mrs. McCready were no more, and meanwhile, an unremarkable expat couple was living quietly in Jamaica. The guilt of placing them in that position was ever-present in the background of my thoughts, but it was nothing to the guilt I would have felt if they'd come under the magnifying glass of the Committee.

I focused once more on the here-and-now, aware that my mind was wandering—another symptom of approaching heat, though one that I could control well enough as long as I paid attention. Our surroundings out here were downright bleak. It had been more than fifteen minutes since I'd seen a car pass in the other direction. There were likely to be other motorcades using this route, though many of the delegates would have left Bucharest last night and stayed in Târgoviște to avoid the early morning commute.

The car in front of us—the one with Flynn and Alex—slowed.

"What the hell's this?" Jax muttered from the front seat. His hand delved beneath his jacket at the height one might expect to find a shoulder holster, and my pulse quickened. Beside me, Kam straightened in his seat. The driver muttered something in Romanian, slowing as well.

I craned forward, trying to see, and got a confused impression of several off-road vehicles parked some distance away from the roadway ahead of us, nestled among the brownish scrub. Before I could draw breath to ask what was going on, a massive noise deafened me, and the limo went tumbling sideways like a child's toy beneath the force of a fiery explosion.

FOUR

Leona

THE SEATBELT dug into my chest and shoulder, squeezing the breath from my lungs as the car rolled. Metal shrieked around me. The side of my head slammed into the window, my skull predictably proving softer than the bulletproof glass. Pain exploded from the site of impact, my awareness fading to a distant sensation of everything moving around me as my arms and legs lolled, beyond my control.

My vision flared white, then dark. My hearing dulled to a liquid *shush-shush, shush-shush* in time with my heartbeat. When my senses cleared enough to make some kind of sense of my surroundings, I was hanging upside down. Something warm dripped from my temple.

"Leo! *Leo!*" A voice was calling my name from somewhere very close by. I thought maybe it had been calling for a while, and it seemed odd that I hadn't noticed it sooner. Sharp sounds came from somewhere farther away—*rat-a-tat-tat... rat-a-tat-tat*. The combination was loud enough to echo through my aching head and make my ears ring unpleasantly.

A grunt of effort came from next to me, and I turned in time to see a dark shape fall free, landing with a pained yelp on the floor — *roof?* — of the battered metal and glass cage.

The last few minutes gradually reassembled into something that made sense… though my head felt like an overfilled water balloon as gravity dragged too much blood into it. We were in a limo, headed to Târgovişte. The car had flipped over. The noise outside was gunfire. The shape next to me was…

"Kam?" It emerged as a bare rasp.

"*Leo*," Kam gasped.

Hands tugged at the belt holding me suspended upside down, fighting with the release mechanism to no avail. I blinked, trying to bring my surroundings into focus, but the shapes no longer made sense. Where the driver should have been sitting, there was just twisted metal. I blinked, nauseated by the odd delay between my eyes moving and the change of perspective registering in my brain.

The front passenger side door had been sheared away, leaving it open to the outside. The seat was still there, and a burly form hung from it, upside down as I was. The alpha security guard — Jax, my brain helpfully supplied — groaned and coughed. At least he was still alive. Red liquid dripped from his side, landing on the inside of the limo's roof in a steady *plop, plop, plop.*

"We've got to get you free," Kam said tightly. "Leo, damn it—please *say* something!"

"*Ow*," I managed faintly, not able to get enough breath past the constriction of the jammed seatbelt for more.

In the front seat, Jax groaned again, the sound trailing off to a low rumble of discontent. His hands scrabbled weakly at his own chest, with no real coordination. Outside, the skull-rattling sound of automatic weapons fire subsided. I could hear car engines pulling up. It sounded like they were right next to us.

"Oh, god," Kam whispered.

Car doors slammed. Voices filtered through the gaps where parts of the car had been ripped away, but I couldn't understand what was being said. The words made no sense. It was a foreign language, but not Romanian. Turkish, maybe?

I blinked stupidly, still hanging from the seat like a landed fish. The muzzle of a gun entered through the missing passenger door, pointed directly at Jax's face.

"Don't shoot," Kam said. "Please. They're injured."

It was the same calm voice he'd been using when I'd returned from dancing at the party last night to find Kostya Nikolayev looming over him—the one that meant he was barely holding it together.

The gunman used the muzzle of the pistol to nudge Jax's cheek roughly. The alpha moaned, but did not stir otherwise. The man withdrew, and a loud, fast-paced conversation ensued. Within seconds, the limo rocked beneath us as hands tugged and yanked at the mostly intact backseat door on Kam's side until it creaked open on protesting hinges.

Kam immediately lifted his hands in surrender, placing his body in front of mine. "They're injured," he said again, and then repeated the words in French. Two men dragged him out through the half-open door. As he disappeared from my field of view, a spike of fear finally managed to penetrate the woolen blanket of shock smothering my emotions.

In the front of the limo, a man sawed away at the seatbelt restraining Jax's body, until he finally fell free with a thump. Another slid into the back seat and started doing the same thing to my seatbelt. I made out several people pulling the alpha out of the car, clearly struggling with his muscular bulk. Then my belt gave way and I tumbled down, the sudden jolt of hitting the roof too much for my wavering consciousness to deal with.

Darkness claimed me, even as a rough hand closed around my ankle and started to drag me out of the door.

The next time I woke, there was a heavy bag tied over my head, and whatever hard surface I was sprawled on was jouncing and jolting. I could hear engine noise, and that sparked a vague memory of off-road vehicles.

Panic slithered through my guts, but a familiar smooth-skinned hand was tangled with mine.

Kam.

I squeezed his fingers, and heard him catch his breath before he squeezed back convulsively. A moment later, the vehicle hit a massive bump. My stomach dipped, and awareness fled once more.

Consciousness came in fits and starts after that. Kam was always there, the clammy sweat of fear slicking our skin where his hand clasped mine. Eventually, the darkness grew complete as my mind apparently gave up the fight for a bit. When I came to, the bag and the engine noise were gone. The hard surface beneath me no longer swayed and bounced.

The air was faintly chilly, damp with humidity and the smell of stone. Kam's fingers were no longer tangled with mine, and that was enough to send me struggling upright, trying to blink my vision into focus despite the sharp, throbbing ache in my temple.

"She's awake." The hoarse voice came from somewhere off to my left. It sounded vaguely familiar, but I couldn't place it.

Footsteps scuffled, and someone crouched next to me, a hand coming to rest on my shoulder. "*Leo.*"

I relaxed. "Kam. Where…?" The rest of the words caught in my dry throat, making me cough.

"Don't try to talk yet," he said softly. "Stay put for a minute—I'll get you some water."

I tried to take in my surroundings as he pushed up from the floor and crossed to the other side of the dimly lit space. Three of the walls appeared to be natural rock, and the floor was packed dirt. The fourth wall looked like plaster… or maybe concrete? It had a heavy-looking metal door set in the middle. A small, barred opening at head height let in the only light—the harsh sodium-yellow glow of a light bulb hanging from the ceiling outside.

Another figure sat slumped against the far wall. Gradually, my omega eyesight sharpened, adjusting to the dimness, and I recognized our alpha escort, Jax. His gaze met mine, impossibly blue, but dulled by a sheen of pain and weakness.

Kam returned, crouching beside me with a bucket and a ladle. I tried to look him over, but he was backlit from the light in the hallway.

"Are you hurt?" I rasped. Everything was hazy, but I had a vague memory of a spectacular car wreck.

"I'm fine," he said. "Just sore and bruised. Drink this, but don't blame me if you get dysentery or something in a few days."

At this point, I would have drunk muddy ditch water if it meant getting some moisture back in my mouth and throat. I steadied the ladle he lifted for me and sipped, covering a grimace. This… might have *been* muddy ditch water, actually. It was stale tasting and unappealingly lukewarm. I swallowed carefully until the desperate edge disappeared from my thirst.

"Where are we?" I asked. My eyes wandered back to the alpha in the room, and I frowned. "Jax? That's your name, right? You're injured. How badly?"

A bunch of half-formed thoughts and memories buzzed around my head like angry flies. I had a feeling that when they finally swarmed me, it would be… *bad.*

"I took metal shrapnel from the limo in my left arm and side, Madam Ambassador," Jax said. "It will be all right once I can dig it out and get the bleeding stopped. Alphas are hard to kill."

"I'll try to help you with that as soon as I make sure Leo's okay," Kam said.

It was matter-of-fact. Jax seemed to accept it, even though he had no way of knowing the horrors that Kam had seen as a youth in the omega breeding pens. All he would see was a pretty, soft-spoken and slightly effeminate beta diplomatic attaché.

"Thank you," said the alpha. "And although you've got no reason to think all that highly of us after what happened this morning, you should both know that no one will hurt either of you while I'm still breathing. The others will come and extract us as soon as they can."

The buzzing memories settled into place. I'd been right—it was bad.

I swallowed convulsively, and focused on pulling my shit together. "Right. I'm sure they will." *If they're even still alive*, I didn't add. Clearing my throat, I continued, "Don't be in such a hurry to throw your life away in the meantime, though. Getting yourself killed won't do anything to keep us safe."

Jax clenched his jaw stubbornly, but he didn't correct me. He had to know I was right, after all.

"My pack will come for us," he repeated, rather than contradicting me.

"Do we know who the kidnappers are, or what they're after?" Kam asked. He tilted my head toward the inadequate light coming from the hallway, and peeled my eyelids back one at a time, staring at the pupils.

"Same size, I hope?" I asked dryly, well aware of the protocol for suspected concussion.

"As far as I can tell," he said.

"They were speaking Turkish earlier," Jax mused. "Separatists, maybe."

"I'm pretty sure at least some of them understand French," Kam said. "Do you speak Turkish?"

"Only a few phrases," Jax replied. "Mostly curse words and insults, if I'm being honest."

"If they speak French, we can communicate if we need to," I told him. "Assuming they decide to listen to us, of course."

"I wouldn't get my hopes up on that front, ma'am," Jax said.

Unfortunately, I suspected he was right about that.

"Do we have any idea where we physically are?" I asked. "This place is underground—I can tell that much."

"I'm afraid I was unconscious during transport," Jax said stiffly, sounding like he blamed himself for not magically overcoming his injuries sooner.

"I wasn't," Kam said. "They tied bags over our heads, so I've got no idea on direction, but this is a cave system in the mountains—possibly a retrofitted mine. It has to be in the Southern Carpathians, I'm pretty sure. The drive only lasted an hour or two."

"Paved roads?" Jax asked. "Or dirt?"

"No roads, at least for a good chunk of it," Kam told him. "Bad roads for the rest. I'm sorry—I couldn't tell if they were paved or not, but there were lots of potholes."

Jax nodded, shifting in place against the rocky wall, only to flinch as he aggravated his wounds. His ambergris and cypress scent soured, and my omega hindbrain helpfully poured stress hormones into my system in response. I tamped down the urge to stumble upright on shaky legs and go try to comfort him.

"Kam," I said instead. "I'm okay. Go help Jax get patched up as best you can, all right?"

I had no doubt Kam was fighting the same urges I was, when it came to the magnetic male sitting on the other side of the cell. He nodded and gave my shoulder a reassuring squeeze before rising stiffly to his feet and heading over to join our resident injured alpha.

"Can you stand?" he asked. "The best light will be right by the door, and we'll need to get a proper look at the situation. It might be better to leave the shrapnel alone if pulling it out would cause too much additional bleeding."

Jax grunted and levered himself upright. Kam helped him out of his torn and filthy suit jacket, easing it off his injured arm. The white button-down shirt followed. It was stained red, and so was the white undershirt beneath it. He'd lost quite a bit of blood—but, as he'd said himself, alphas were hard to kill.

I clung to that knowledge and tore my eyes away when he reached back with his good hand, grasping the torn undershirt and pulling it over his head in a single, smooth movement. Injured or no, a shirtless, muscular alpha was not something I needed to see right now. Not so close to—

My mind blanked out in a moment of perfect, crystal-clear denial.

Not so close to my heat.

Oh, god. My heat was only days away, and I was trapped in a cell with an unfamiliar alpha, at the mercy of kidnappers who might want us as hostages, or for ransom money, or...

Trapped. I was *trapped*.

In a cell.

With my heat coming on.

Cold sweat broke out across my entire body, my heartbeat thundering into triple time. My head pounded in counterpoint to my galloping pulse as sudden panic gripped me. Jax turned to look at me, a frown creasing his sharply chiseled features as though he'd heard my breathing pick up and my heart thumping against my ribcage like a trapped animal.

And... of *course* he'd heard it. He was an alpha, and the cell wasn't that large. Kam looked up from his examination of the bloody tear in Jax's side, following the alpha's gaze to me. Something must have shown in my expression. I'd probably gone pale as a sheet, all the blood draining from my face.

"Leona?" he asked, worry sharpening his tone. "What is it? What's wrong?"

FIVE

Leona

"MY LUGGAGE," I said stupidly. "Is our luggage here?"

Understanding flooded Kam's features, followed by horror. He hid both reactions under a poker face within seconds.

"No," Jax said blankly. "I… don't think our luggage was really top of mind for the terrorists who planted an I.E.D. and snatched us from a diplomatic motorcade on a public highway. Why? I take it there was something important in your suitcase?"

I opened my mouth and paused, stuck for a reply.

Kam looked between us and promptly rescued me. "She… takes medication. For a chronic condition."

"What kind of condition?" Jax asked, because apparently we were going to have this conversation with me staring at his bare chest and the jagged hunk of metal protruding from his sluggishly bleeding side.

"It's personal," I replied weakly. "I don't like to talk about it."

Mainly because talking about it could get me killed, I thought.

"It'll be fine for a few days," Kam said, the tension in his shoulders belying his calm tone. "I'm sure the cavalry will show up before it becomes an issue."

I forced down my panic, grabbing the lifeline he'd just thrown. "Yes," I agreed. "Sorry. It'll be fine. Don't mind me. How bad is that?" I added by way of deflection, gesturing to the ugly wound in Jax's side.

The alpha craned to look at it.

"Better out than in, probably," he said, and reached around with his uninjured arm as though he was going to yank the piece of metal out of his side with no further discussion.

Kam batted his hand away. "Let me. And give me that undershirt—we'll use it to keep pressure on the wound until the bleeding stops."

"You know, that old 'better out than in' thing refers to alcohol," I said weakly. "Not shrapnel."

Jax glanced over at me, his brow furrowing. "Same principal, isn't it?"

"Ugh. *Alphas*," Kam muttered, and tugged the metal free.

The alpha in question didn't even flinch. Kam tossed the piece of shrapnel into the corner, where it bounced against the rocky wall with a light clink before falling to the dirt floor. He pressed the balled-up undershirt against the wound, which was oozing blood but not spurting.

My eyes slid away. Unlike Kam, I'd led a remarkably sheltered life for an omega. I'd always passed as beta... never had to endure the ugliness of subjugated life directly. Before today, the most blood I'd ever seen outside of a movie screen was a bleeding finger after a kitchen knife accident.

My fellow omega had directed his erstwhile patient to keep pressure on the first wound while he twisted Jax's other arm into the weak light, peering at his bulging bicep.

"If the other piece is still in there, it's buried too deep to do anything about," he said.

"It's still in there," Jax said. "But don't worry about it."

"At least it's small," Kam offered.

"Yeah," Jax agreed. "It'll be fine. I can still fight if I have to."

"Nobody's fighting anyone," I said, trying to channel authority into my tone. "We'll talk to them. Negotiate. Find out what they want and try to come to some sort of understanding. I am supposed to be a diplomat, after all."

"The others will find us soon." Jax spoke the words as though they were an unbreakable maxim, and I didn't try to argue.

"Sure," I said. "Until then, we just need to keep it nice and low-key, all right? Let Kam and me do the talking. Everything will be fine."

I wasn't sure who I was trying to reassure—me, Kam, or the injured alpha who seemed to be psyching himself up for a one-sided kamikaze battle against armed terrorists.

* * *

As it happened, there were no more opportunities for diplomatic discussion than there were for physical fights. Time was difficult to track beneath the unchanging light from the single bulb in the corridor outside, but based on my hunger and the hours I'd slept, I was pretty sure a full day passed before the lock on the door clanked.

It swung open just far enough to reveal a beta man holding an AR-15 pointed at Jax's head. Kam and I froze. Jax just glared at him, unblinking and unimpressed. The man shifted to make enough space for another of our kidnappers to drop a fresh bucket of water inside the door, followed a moment later by a tray.

"Let me talk to you for a moment," I said in French. "Can you understand me?"

The men withdrew and the door slammed shut.

I sighed. "You try next time, Kam."

"Sure," he said listlessly. "I'll give it a shot."

Jax went and wordlessly retrieved the tray of food—bread and dried brown strips of something. Jerky, maybe. My empty stomach churned with nervous worry, but I ate my portion anyway, washing it down with some of the stale water.

The situation was maddening, and it was all I could do to contain my growing panic. We were in a cell perhaps fifteen feet by twenty feet. It was bare, except for a latrine pit. A rough wooden box sat over it, with a hole cut from the top for use as a seat. We had a single threadbare blanket to share between us. Jax had waved it off when I tried to give it to him several hours earlier, so Kam and I had wrapped up in it to sleep when exhaustion overcame us.

My head still ached, though it was getting better quickly. *Too* quickly. I knew I would need to play up the injury for at least another few days, to cover the fact that my pre-heat omega hormones were supercharging the healing process. I'd been knocked unconscious. A beta wouldn't have bounced back from this kind of head wound so easily. I could only hope the grime on my face would distract from the speed at which the bruise was fading.

Jax had fared quite a bit worse than I had in the crash. The shrapnel wound in his side had stopped bleeding after a couple of hours, but the left half of his face was bruised badly enough that even alpha healing would take some time. More worrying, the other piece of shrapnel was still buried in his arm, too deep to pull out without some kind of tweezers or forceps. Infection was almost a certainty—and while Jax hadn't been lying when he said alphas were hard to kill, that didn't mean *impossible* to kill.

Despite his quiet confidence that rescue would be on its way soon, the hours dragged on with no sign of anything going on outside of our little prison, for either good or ill.

The worst part of it was, I desperately needed some kind of a contingency plan, and yet I couldn't say a single word about my heat. Without Jax's presence, Kam and I might at least have tried to brainstorm some kind of damage control. With him here, I didn't dare speak about it, except in the vaguest possible terms regarding my 'lost medication.'

I needed pills that I didn't have. There was no way to get them. If enough time passed without them, it would be *bad*. None of this was helpful in the least. And indeed, as the clock ticked inevitably toward my oncoming heat, rescue still might not be enough to avert my own personal disaster.

One didn't simply run down to the local pharmacy to buy heat suppressors. Getting them without being caught was a complicated and expensive process. If the cavalry showed up and pulled us out of here an hour from now, I still wouldn't be able to get them in time unless my luggage had miraculously survived the crash and someone thought to bring it along during the rescue operation.

My only possible hope would be to disappear into some remote bolthole, where I could hide myself away before I started perfuming.

Because once I did, it would advertise my omega-in-heat status to every single person in my vicinity who had a nose.

I *desperately* didn't want to have to ride out a heat cycle alone. And it was probably moot, anyway—I didn't have a clue how I could find a safe hideout in an unfamiliar country during the aftermath of a terrorist kidnapping. Even after we were rescued, I'd be under constant watch. Medical checks. Debriefing. Round the clock guards. There was no way I'd be able to hide what was going on.

Time ticked on, inexorable. I marked it by my companions' periods of sleep... by the guards' infrequent deliveries of bad food and stale water.

By the slow slide of my body toward disaster.

Days passed. The guards wouldn't talk to any of us, in any of the languages we knew. In desperation, I even had Jax curse at them in halting Turkish.

Nothing.

Dark smudges of worry and exhaustion were growing beneath Kam's eyes. He knew exactly what was at stake...exactly how few options I had left. I was certain that the time when I would normally have taken the heat blocker had come and gone, as the hours and days marched slowly by. My pheromone suppressors would be giving up the fight within the next twenty-four hours, at most. And... what then?

Unless Jax succumbed to some kind of blood infection bad enough to render him unconscious, he would figure out what was happening immediately. I knew almost nothing about him beyond the obvious. He was subjugated. Chemically castrated—so at least if someone raped me, it would be our beta captors and not him. He seemed like a pleasant and respectful enough individual—now, at least. But alphas had a reputation. Yes, it was a stereotype… but with the sheltered beta life I'd led, I didn't know enough alphas personally to know how much of that stereotype was bounded in truth.

In fact—sad as it was—my interaction with Jax, Flynn, and Alex was the closest contact I'd ever knowingly had with alphas. Maybe there had been others hiding in plain sight like Kam and I were. If so, they'd been doing a good enough job that I'd been none the wiser.

It hardly mattered, though. Whether or not Jax turned into a caveman at the first whiff of my pheromones, once the guards came in to find me writhing on the floor and flooding the cell with heat-scent, it would all be over. They would either kill me—with or without including some combination of torture and gang rape first—or they'd try to use me as some kind of leverage against my government. And I had little doubt the UFNA would cheerfully hand me over to the Committee for trial and execution as an unregistered omega, if it came down to it. Otherwise, the scandal would rock the parliamentary government to its core.

I was pacing, scratching absently at my forearms with my fingernails. I wanted to disappear into the dirt floor... to climb the stone walls and hide in a crevice like a rat. I needed to get away. I needed to be somewhere else. *Anywhere* else.

"Madam Ambassador," Jax said, his manner still perfectly formal and proper despite several days spent huddled on a bare dirt floor nursing untreated wounds. "I know there's something you two aren't telling me, and I think it's time you did. Is it to do with your medical condition, or is there something else?"

Kam's shoulders hunched a little tighter, and he ran a nervous hand through his dark hair. I was spared having to come up with an answer by the sound of the lock on the cell door releasing. Irrational desperation drove me toward it as it opened. I rushed at the two familiar guards, heedless of the semi-automatic rifle in my face. In my peripheral vision, I was dimly aware of Jax hauling himself to his feet... of Kam gasping my name in warning.

"Please," I begged the guards, forgetting to speak in French as my blood buzzed and itched in my veins. "Please, you have to let me out of here! I can't be in this cell—"

The one with the AR-15 used the barrel to shove me roughly backward. I stumbled and hit the ground in a sprawl. The impact jarred my brain loose of its heat-daze in the same instant Jax growled and gathered himself to lunge.

"*No!*" I cried, as the rifle swung around to cover the enraged alpha. "*Shit!* Jax, stand *down!*"

Jax clenched his fists at his sides in frustration, but he planted his feet and did not charge.

"Just… sit down, Jax. Please." Kam spoke in his calmest voice. His body language was open and appeasing—the kind of posture every omega knew how to employ instinctively from early childhood. He switched to French, keeping the same even tone as he spoke to the guards. "We're calm now. There's no need for violence."

"Violence is how we make change." The new voice came from the open doorway, speaking awkward, heavily accented English.

He strode in, unfamiliar, but dressed in the same mix of local clothing style and military surplus gear as the guards. His air of command was obvious.

"Please," I told him. "We need to talk to you. We can come to some kind of arrangement…"

He ignored me, and tossed a battered notebook on the ground in front of us.

"You and you." He pointed first at Kam, then at me. "Learn this speech. Tomorrow we make video."

"If you want money, our government will pay," I tried desperately, knowing it was a lie.

Knowing I was throwing away every ounce of dignity I had left by even saying the words. What must Kam think of me right now? What must Jax think?

The leader ignored me. "Learn speech, or we torture you."

He turned and left without a backward glance. The others followed him, the gunman backing out cautiously, with his eyes fixed on Jax the whole time. The door slammed shut. They hadn't left us food or water.

I curled forward, burying my face in my hands.

"What's in the notebook?" Jax asked. "This is bad, but the details might give us a better idea of *how* bad."

I let my hands fall to my lap. Kam must have realized I was too far gone to manage even such a simple action. He slipped past me and picked up the notebook, taking it to the door to make use of the limited light. I watched listlessly as he flipped through the pages from front to back, my skin feeling too tight and too hot.

He flipped back to the beginning and scanned the pages more slowly, his brows drawing together. When he was done, he swallowed and cleared his throat. "It's… uh…"

"Just read it," I said. "Don't try to sugarcoat things."

Kam swallowed again. "First we're supposed to say our names. Then, 'We have been taken prisoner by the glorious forces of the Beta Liberation Front, and will be executed for our government's crimes against beta supremacy.'" My heart sank. "'Even now,'" Kam continued, "'right-thinking beta scientists are perfecting a weapon that will eliminate the alphomic threat once and for all. When it is ready, the whole world will know.' And then there's some BS about how wonderful the terrorists are and how we totally decided to support their cause despite the fact that they're going to cut our heads off."

It was all I could do not to break down weeping on the spot. I could barely think, the entire situation was already poised to go down in flames the moment Jax caught a whiff of my oncoming heat... and now we also had to come up with a way to keep from getting executed, while somehow preventing a terror organization from producing a weapon of mass destruction for use against our people.

It was impossible. It *could not be done*, and all thanks to a vicious joke of biology.

This disaster was going to be my fault. My responsibility.

"I can't do this," I murmured, barely audible. "Oh, god—Kam. I'm *so sorry*. I can't stop this."

Our eyes met. He heard the words I wasn't saying, and the same agony shone in his eyes as was doubtless shining in mine.

"Let's not panic," Jax said after an awkward moment—and abrupt, incandescent anger flooded me in all its irrational, hormonal glory.

"We're going to die," I ground out, biting the words off one by one. "A lot of other people are *going to die*. And where the hell is your team? Your *pack*, that was supposed to magically appear and rescue us?"

"*Leo*," Kam warned.

"They'll come," Jax said with a perfect, serene complacency that only fueled my anger. "I have faith in them. But in the meantime, let me take a look at that notebook, Mr. Patel."

Kam handed it over, while my impotent, unreasonable anger twisted around to point firmly inward. I *hated* this. I hated the knowledge that I was losing control of my mind, my emotions... my body. My clothing felt like it was made of nettles. Clammy sweat was breaking out across my back. I was about to plunge into what would be the worst, most horrific day of my tragically short life, and I'd be dragging the others along for the ride before we all died.

My sex began to throb and ache with emptiness. Any moment now, I'd start to manufacture slick. I choked down a moan and crawled to the section of wall where the lone blanket in the cell lay in a crumpled heap, wrapping it around myself to form a pathetic, threadbare cocoon. Kam closed his eyes and bowed his head. Jax shot me a sharp look of concern before visibly recalling himself to the notebook. The faint scent of honey and orange blossom rose around me, and I pulled the blanket tighter.

"There's nothing else written in the book," Jax was saying. "The light's not really good enough to see if there are indentations from writing on other pages that might have been torn out, but…"

He trailed off, nostrils flaring as he scented the air. An instant later, the alpha's eyes landed on me like a physical weight. My entire body tightened. Black market pheromone suppressors gave up the ghost beneath the onslaught, as my scent glands pumped out perfume in fragrant clouds.

My heat had begun.

SIX

Leona

"YOU'RE..." JAX BEGAN, his eyes losing focus as he breathed in deeply. "You're an..."

Kam moved in front of me, blocking my view of the alpha on the far side of the cell. "She's a UFNA ambassador, and you're part of her security team."

He was trying to sound confident. Commanding. To my ears, he mostly just sounded terrified.

"How in the *hell* did you manage to make it to a posting this high?" Jax asked, obviously bewildered.

"By being very good at her job," Kam snapped.

I peered around Kam's legs, succumbing to a deep-seated need to keep the alpha in my line of sight. Blue eyes locked with mine, and he took a step toward us, as though drawn by a string. Kam jerked a hand up—arm straight, palm out. He squared his shoulders, trying to make himself seem bigger.

"No. Stop right there. Take a step back."

Kam put on a good show, but I knew him well enough to hear the faint tremor behind his words. A thread of rational thought pierced the haze of fever and emptiness smothering me. My sweet and gentle omega packmate was planning to stand between me and an alpha who could break him in half like a twig.

"Kam, don't," I begged.

The alpha across from us was breathing heavily, his scent thickening in response to mine. I had to think... I had to push past my body's growing neediness. Every nerve thrummed, attuned to the figure on the other side of the cell. His dark, woodsy aroma flooded my senses, threatening to drown me.

But there was something...

Something important...

"Jax," Kam said carefully. "You can't help her, regardless. Even if she wanted it, you're not in a position to —"

"Yes, I am." The alpha's voice had deepened to a basso rumble. "Step aside. Let her speak for herself."

Subjugated. That was what Kam was trying to say... what my muddled brain had been reaching for. Subjugated alphas were chemically castrated.

Kam shot me a worried look over his shoulder. He must have seen some shred of coherence still in my gaze, because he reluctantly moved a step to the side. Jax stood before me, solid and strong and overwhelmingly *alpha*. My entire body clenched, the muscles of my aching passage cramping painfully. I curled around the agonizing emptiness, still holding eye contact.

The person behind those blue eyes and that irresistible scent was a stranger. And I was a thirty-one-year-old omega virgin who—thanks to years of using heat blockers—had experienced exactly *one* natural heat cycle before now. I was trapped in a cell and facing execution. The thought of his touch—when I would be too weak to resist and too mindless with need to communicate with him—terrified me.

I held his gaze despite my trembling muscles, fighting the urge that made me want to crawl to him on my hands and knees and lick my way up his body an inch at a time.

"Don't touch me," I choked out. "*I do not give you permission.*"

Blue eyes burned. My vision narrowed until they were all I could focus on. After a moment, the alpha firmed his jaw and nodded.

"I understand," he said. "This is going to be a really bad twenty-four hours, Madam Ambassador—but I'll do everything in my power to protect both of you when the guards return in the morning."

A tiny thread of relief cut through my clamoring nerves. I knew I was also supposed to be worrying about tomorrow, but the threat of execution was already growing distant and unimportant compared to the storm raging inside my body.

"Thank you," Kam murmured in abject relief, and I didn't think he was only talking about the promise of protection.

"We're still looking at a deeply unpleasant night for everyone involved," Jax said.

"Followed by one hell of an unpleasant day," Kam agreed. "Probably a fatal one. We know. I mean it, though. Thank you."

Jax visibly fought his instincts, and forced himself to step back and reclaim his seat against the far wall. He slid down and rested his forearms on his raised knees.

"Alphas aren't animals," he said. "Despite what you may have heard."

Kam cautiously settled down next to me. "I didn't mean to imply you were. I apologize if it came across that way."

I tried to draw comfort from my packmate's familiar presence at my side, but my body didn't want another omega right now. He kept a careful inch of space between us, and I wasn't sure if his touch would help me or make everything a hundred times worse. Miserably, I huddled deeper into the blanket and shuddered, trying and failing not to shoot darting glances toward the person my body really craved.

Jax looked back at me frankly. "Please tell me you've at least ridden out heats before. Do you understand what you're in for?"

"Yes," I snapped, knowing it was a lie. Being trapped in a confined space with an alpha changed everything—and things had been bad enough the first time, almost fifteen years previously, when I'd had to ride it out on my own. This? This was a whole new level of misery.

"All right," he said, accepting it.

"Leo," Kam said softly. "Do you want me closer? Or should I give you space?"

I don't know, I thought, more than a little desperately. *I want this not to be happening.*

"Just… stay where you are, please?" I managed in a shaking voice. "For now, anyway."

"Okay," he said. "I'll be right here." With a deep breath—one that did nothing to ease the tension rolling off his body in waves—he turned back to Jax. "What about you? Have *you* ridden out an omega's heat before?"

"Oh, yeah," Jax said. "Way too many times. I was a breeder for years in the slave pens. Sometimes the omegas were still too weak from their last litters when the plantation owners threw them back into the whelping rotation. Getting pupped again before they were recovered from their last litter could be fatal, so we'd sit out the heat and get through it as best we could."

"I didn't realize you came from the plantations," Kam replied. "Didn't the overseers punish you for defying them like that?"

Jax gave a humorless laugh. "I imagine it was a bit of a catch-22 from their perspective. Fertility rates plummet if an omega doesn't have privacy and a sense of safety during heat. That privacy gave us enough freedom to wriggle out of breeding when it would have been too dangerous. Mostly, I think the fact that it helped keep the overall mortality rates lower meant they let it slide."

Kam had almost ended up in those same breeding pens, I thought distantly. *If he hadn't been too stubborn... too intractable. If his owners hadn't decided to sterilize him and throw him into the slave auctions instead —*

My lower abdomen cramped again, and I swallowed a moan. I pictured the pups he might have produced... how beautiful they would have been. Unlike him, I'd never wanted to carry. I lacked his innate optimism for the future. How could I justify bringing new lives into a world as broken as ours?

Now, though, my body didn't care about the future, and I hated it for the way it craved breeding, craved pregnancy—craved all the things *that I didn't want, damn it.*

"Sometimes walking can help with the cramps," Jax offered. "For a while, anyway."

I couldn't seem to rally words to reply, and I didn't think my knees would hold me, so I only shook my head and buried my face in the stinking blanket. At least it distracted me from the smell of cypress and ambergris, even if it couldn't block my own sickly-sweet perfume.

There was nothing to do except try to tough it out.

I lasted maybe an hour, at most.

"Please," I sobbed, writhing in Kam's arms. I was on fire. Any minute now, it would consume me whole. "I was wrong. I lied! Please, alpha—I need your knot. It hurts! I'm so empty, I can't..."

Jax groaned—a low noise that ricocheted through my body like a shot, raising gooseflesh in its wake. I leaned toward that rough sound of desire, my nipples hardening into painful points.

"Leona," Kam said. "Try to hold on. Just a little longer, all right?"

He'd wrapped me up against his body when I'd first started crying—still cocooned in the ratty blanket. As I'd feared, his touch was both better and worse than no touch at all.

"Alpha, *please*," I begged.

"Heat blockers," Jax muttered. "Damn it."

The words made no sense. I didn't *want* his words. I wanted his *knot*.

"What about them?" Kam asked, still keeping me trapped against him.

"She uses them?" Jax asked. "Well, she'd have to, I guess."

"Obviously," Kam said, a bit sharply. I whimpered in distress, and he shushed me, immediately contrite.

Jax met my eyes. "Madam Ambassador. *Leona.* Heat blockers make your rebound heat stronger."

Kam caught his breath. "She's been on them for years."

Another sob of frustration escaped me. They kept *talking* and *talking*, when all I needed was a knot to fill up the empty void inside me that was sucking me inside out like a black hole. I felt like I was burning, all the moisture in my body boiling itself away in the form of sweat and slick.

"This isn't going to work." Jax dragged a hand over his face. It was shaking. "Her temperature could spike high enough to do permanent damage. We need to do something different."

There was a pause, and Kam's voice sounded horribly uncertain when he spoke. "Were you telling the truth before, about being able to help her? Aren't you on the alpha drug regimen?"

"I was telling the truth, yes—but that's not what I meant." Jax sounded like he was barely holding it together, and I thought maybe, if I could just get my arms and legs free of the damned blanket so I could present for him...? "I've got no problem with an omega changing their mind and stopping a mating during their heat," he went on. "But when a 'no' becomes a 'yes' during a cycle this intense, it's not a real 'yes.' Also, there's the matter of contraceptives. If she's using blockers, I'm guessing she's not on them—and while these aren't great conditions for getting pupped, it's still a possibility."

The words flowed over me without sticking. I couldn't follow the meaning of the exchange, but Kam flinched hard against me.

"No," he said, the whisper barely audible. "No, she's not." I felt him swallow hard. "This could kill her, couldn't it."

Another pause. "It's possible. I know tomorrow's going to bring its own set of problems. But that doesn't mean I want to take that kind of chance tonight."

"Then… what?" Kam demanded. "What exactly are you suggesting?"

The alpha sighed. "She needs a knot. So, the question is, exactly how close are you two?"

SEVEN

Kameron

I BLINKED AT the hulking alpha seated across the room from us. Leo squirmed in my arms, restless and feverish. She was smearing slick against my dress slacks, one of her thighs splayed across my lap.

"I'm… pretty sure I don't have the equipment to do that particular job," I said blankly, my mind shying away from thinking about the scarred wreck that had once been my omegan reproductive system.

"That's not an answer," Jax pointed out, with more patience than I would have expected from an alpha stuck in a cell with an omega in heat, and a perceived male beta who was barely keeping his shit together. "You knew her secret. You were ready to stand up to an alpha twice your size to protect her. Are you together?"

"It's complicated," I said, still feeling like there was a two-second disconnect between my brain and my mouth.

"Here and now, it's really not," Jax shot back, a hint of an alpha bark creeping into his tone. "Have you been intimate with each other, yes or no?"

My spine snapped straight beneath that tone. I had to resist the instinct to roll my head to the side and look away, baring my throat.

"Yes," I hissed. "Which doesn't change the fact that I can't help her with this. I can't get hard, all right? If I could fix this for her, *don't you think I already would have?*"

I could feel the defensive claws coming out, and I cursed myself when Leo whimpered in my arms and began to cry again. I tried to swallow everything down—to project calm support rather than the clammy terror that was choking me like a noose.

"You have hands," Jax said flatly. "So you're going to provide the knot, and I'm going to stay over here and provide the pheromones. It's still not the kind of consent that an omega deserves, but at least it's not getting fucked by a stranger."

Or dying.

The words hung in the air, unspoken.

I fought to settle my churning stomach. After a moment, I managed to shove the fear down far enough to stroke Leo's sweaty hair away from her brow. The bruise on her temple from the car wreck had almost completely faded, I noticed distantly.

"*Odama,*" I whispered. "We're going to try to help you."

"Alpha, please," she whined, rutting mindlessly against my leg. "Need the alpha! Please, *please*..."

I was weeping silently, tears tracking down my cheeks. Fool that I was, I'd always pictured us going out in a blaze of glory when our secret finally came out—making some kind of noble, defiant speech to the television cameras as we were hauled away, swaying hearts and minds everywhere to our cause. Because, of course, that fantasy was so much more comforting than the reality where we were kidnapped by terrorists, and our captors showed up in the morning to find Leo writhing on the floor, begging for sex.

"Mr. Patel. She needs you to be strong right now, okay?"

I had no idea how Jax was keeping it together... how he was managing to speak in a way that made it clear he actually gave a shit about what the two of us were going through.

"Call me Kam," I told him unsteadily. "I think we entered first-name territory a while ago."

"Kam," he said, and in that instant I wanted nothing more than for the alpha to come over here and wrap both of us up in his strong arms, blocking out the world. I set the ridiculous desire aside forcefully.

"Sorry," I said. "You're right, of course. If you think it will work, that's what we need to do. She'll understand. I'm sure she will."

I tried to believe it.

"Sometimes," Jax said, "there are situations where you can only control a very small number of things. Right now, we can try to ease her heat before it endangers her health. We can't do anything about the rest of it at the moment. But we can do this."

"I hear you." I cleared my throat. "Leo, we're going to help you, okay?"

She whined again and mumbled something, but the words didn't make sense. At this point, approaching her first peak, it was apparent she'd lost the power of speech. Instead, she twisted and writhed, struggling to get free of my embrace.

"She's trying to turn over so she can present," Jax said calmly. "Let her go, Kam."

I let her go, my arms feeling empty the moment I did. Sure enough, Leo rolled onto all fours, panting softly as her back arched in an omega's instinctual lordosis. Presenting for sex to the alpha in the room… begging to be filled.

"When you say 'knot,'" I began uncertainly, because this was nothing the two of us had ever done before. There'd been no point in trying. Outside of heat and in the absence of alpha pheromones, penetration wouldn't be pleasurable in the least for her. For me, it wasn't even an option any more.

"Work as many fingers into her as will comfortably fit," Jax said bluntly. "That probably means either three or four. When I say so, and not before, curl them like you're making a fist and keep them like that." He paused. "I'm sincerely hoping that your nails are short."

"They are," I whispered.

The blanket had slipped from Leo's body to land on the dirt floor. She'd shed her suit jacket when the fever started, and her conservative blouse was partially unbuttoned, hanging off one shoulder after her repeated attempts to wriggle out of her clothing. The dove gray pencil skirt—streaked with filth and blood from the car wreck—had hitched up around her hips when she'd climbed half into my lap earlier. Her light green panties were soaked from the river of slick she'd been putting out for the last hour.

She was as beautiful as she always was, but I knew she wouldn't want to be seen like this. Not under these circumstances. My heart ached for her. Hell, my heart ached for both of us. I tossed the blanket over her back, draping it so it hid her lower body from view as I knelt behind her, silently cursing myself, the terrorists, and the world we'd been born into.

"Leo, I'm going to touch you now," I said. "Just my fingers, but Jax says it will feel like a knot. He's here, but he's going to stay a little distance away and lend you his pheromones, all right? I'm going to move your underwear out of the way. If you want me to stop, shake your head, or say no, or even just move away, and I will, I promise."

It was useless. Stupid. She couldn't understand me in her current condition. She wasn't going to resist my touch, because her body was flooded with industrial-strength heat hormones, and she *couldn't* resist. My words were only a salve to myself, not to her.

"You're a good friend to her," Jax said quietly, from his position across the cell.

"No," I replied, my voice shaking. "I'm really not."

I was a coward. Broken. But right now, my cowardice translated into an unbearable fear of losing her before it was absolutely unavoidable. If we were both going to die, then we were both going to die. It was the prospect of losing her and being left alone to face the monsters that truly chilled my blood. I wormed my right hand under the blanket and hooked Leo's panties down to her thighs. She immediately moaned and pushed her ass into the light touch.

"Listen to me, Leona," Jax said, in that low alpha rumble that pierced straight into the deepest part of an omega's soul. "You're doing so well. We're going to fill you up so good, little *odama*. We'll make all of this go away, and then you can rest for a bit."

I placed one hand on Leo's back to steady her and felt around blindly beneath the blanket with the other, following the trail of slick to its source. No sooner had I gotten lined up than Leo reared back, taking two fingers to the hilt with a keening cry. My throat closed up. She was hot and tight, her passage gripping me with the same rippling muscle that would help her squeeze out pups.

"That's it." Jax's encouragement was quiet. The rasp of a zipper reached my ears. "Sorry about this, by the way. It's the only way to sync our pheromones."

"No, I know," I told him. "It's fine."

It wasn't fine. My back was turned, but I could hear the sound of slapping flesh—the low, ragged sound of uneven breathing. Jax was going to bring himself off, timing his release to coincide with me attempting to trick Leo's body into believing she'd been knotted. His scent would change, and with luck that would trigger Leo's first peak to subside, giving her a respite from the torture of out-of-control hormones rushing around with nowhere to go. Of course, it would also leave Jax with his knot waving in the breeze, which was allegedly a miserable experience for an alpha.

Leo fucked herself shamelessly on my fingers, letting out a series of rhythmic, breathy cries. Her sultry-sweet natural perfume was changing... sharpening. I managed to add a third finger, and finally, a fourth, until that slick, velvety heat was enveloping my hand to the crook of my thumb every time she rocked back.

The sound of Jax's hand on his dick behind me sped up. His scent was changing, too, and I had to fight the urge to look over my shoulder and watch him. The two scents coated my tongue and tickled the back of my throat, making me feel faintly lightheaded. My own vestigial cock twitched, growing heavy and sensitive.

Just the pheromones, I told myself, squeezing my eyes shut and cursing omega biology for the hundredth time in the last hour.

"Get ready," Jax said, sounding decidedly strained.

He grunted, and Leo cried out.

"Now," he said hoarsely. "Do it now."

I bit the inside of my cheek and curled my fingers into a loose fist, wincing at the way Leo's body had to stretch to accommodate the movement. Her muscles clenched and pulsed rhythmically, her back going rigid beneath my other hand. The scent in the cell shifted again—honey and orange melding with musk and cypress to form something new. Something thoroughly intoxicating.

"That's it. Now stay like that until her muscles release you. See if you can ease her down to lie on her side so she can rest easier." Jax's tone sounded exhausted, and I was forcibly reminded of his injuries.

Already, Leo was going boneless. With supreme awkwardness, I managed to direct her sprawl so she was lying in front of me with her back to me, my clenched fingers still inside her. This, unfortunately, had the unintended consequence of putting Jax in my line of sight. He was seated against the rocky wall with one leg drawn up and the other stretched out in front of him, his hand clamped around the knot at the base of his very erect dick.

"Dignity is overrated," he told me, with a wry twist of the lips that couldn't really be called a smile. "That's what I always tell myself, anyway." Lines of strain had settled around the corners of his striking blue eyes.

I tore my gaze away from him in favor of checking on Leo.

"She's dozing," I reported. "Her skin's cooling off; she doesn't feel as feverish."

In my peripheral vision, I saw Jax nod.

"Keep the blanket over her," he said. "In less shit-tastic circumstances than this, she'd have one or more alphas sharing body heat with her while she recovered."

The picture those words conjured up felt like a knife between the ribs. *I'm pretty sure we'd need a bigger nest*, Leo had joked in the Bucharest hotel room, the night before everything had fallen apart. I shifted in place, trying not to jostle her. My skin still felt stretched too tight. My cock still throbbed, half-hard and oversensitive.

Jax watched me, and I had to fight not to squirm beneath his frank regard.

"Oh. You're an omega, too," he said, sounding thoughtful rather than surprised.

"What?" I yelped, my heart thundering into overdrive. *How —* ?

Jax inhaled deeply, his nostrils flaring. "Your pheromone suppressor couldn't keep up — not surprising with another omega in heat in the same enclosed space. You smell like ginger tea with lemon."

"No, that's not—" I began, before cutting myself off and trying to regroup. "I don't take pheromone suppressors. I don't have any reason to!"

Leo made a discontented humming noise in her sleep, her body clenching tighter around my hand. I looked between her and the alpha in the room, caught out and entirely unsure *why*.

"No," Jax said. "I suppose you wouldn't, in the normal course of things. It's barely detectable, even now. You don't have to worry about the betas noticing. They won't." His expression grew troubled. "I guess they got you when you were young, huh? I'm so sorry, Kam. They're monsters. No one should have to go through that."

Twenty years of unaddressed trauma rose up to lodge itself firmly in my throat. I choked, unable to draw breath.

"Blast. I shouldn't have said anything," Jax murmured. "Damned heat-brain. I'm really sorry, Kameron. Just breathe for a minute, okay?"

"It's fine," I rasped, once I'd managed to drag air past the blockage in my chest. Even to my own ears, I sounded about as far from fine as it was possible to get.

"It's not," Jax said. "And neither are you… but that's okay." He was quiet for a moment before continuing. "You're lucky to have each other. Pack is important."

I looked down at Leo, her fiery mane of red hair draped in sweat-soaked tangles. "Yes," I agreed in a tiny voice. "It's everything."

We lapsed into silence.

Eventually, I cleared my throat. "That knot must ache like hell," I observed, forcing my tone into something a bit more normal.

"You aren't kidding," he agreed. "Though maybe not quite as much as you're hand's going to ache by the time she's done with you."

I couldn't dispute it. I'd already lost feeling in my fingers, and the muscles in my forearm were starting to cramp. More time passed, until finally the strong muscles clamped around my hand began to flutter, and finally eased. I cautiously uncurled my fingers and slid them out of Leo's body. She shifted restlessly at the loss, but didn't wake. Relieved, I wiped my hand on a corner of the blanket and shook it out, feeling the tingle of returning blood.

"You should get some rest while you can," Jax said. "She'll start climbing toward the next peak in a few hours. I'll keep watch until then."

Injured or not, he would be good to his word, I knew. Alphas were hardwired to guard omegas during heat, when they were at their most vulnerable. He'd crash afterward, of course, but until Leo's heat markers faded,

Jax's body would consume fat and muscle to sustain a multi-day marathon of no sleep and frequent mating.

He was right, too. I should take advantage of what rest I could get. Feeling shaky—both with reaction to the immediate situation and to other, deeper things—I managed to scoot us both around until I was leaning against the wall with Leo's blanket-wrapped form curled up in my lap. She sighed and nuzzled into me, still smelling of clover honey and orange orchards.

It was so heartbreaking to think of the world depriving itself of the beauty of that scent, forcing her to cover it up to protect herself. I breathed it in deeply, trying to catch a hint of my own perfume intermingled with hers. *Ginger tea with lemon*, Jax had called it. I wasn't sure if I could actually smell it, or if it was mere wishful thinking on my part. Whatever the case, the world at large would never scent me. That knowledge should have been a relief, since it meant my perfume wouldn't give me away.

It wasn't.

"I'm not really an omega," I blurted, the words bubbling up from the depths of my buried self-loathing. "They took it all away... ripped it out by the roots. I'm not... *anything*. Not anymore."

And after tomorrow, I would probably be dead. I wondered if they'd execute us on camera before sending the video to news outlets around the world. I wondered if anyone would mourn me.

"Kameron Patel. Look at me," Jax said, his tone turning steely. I did, instincts responding to that small flexing of alpha power. He lifted his hand to touch his forehead, his eyes holding mine. "If you're an omega here..." His hand moved to rest on his chest, over his heart. "If you're an omega here... then you're still an omega. No one can take that from you. Do you hear me? *No one.*"

My throat closed up again.

"You can be scarred and still be perfect," he went on, his tone solemn. "You can be injured and still be beautiful. And after seeing what you've both accomplished... seeing how you are with each other — you two are without a doubt the most beautiful omegas I've ever met."

My vision blurred as his words sank into me, settling into place. Unable to answer, I hid my face against Leo's hair and held her tight as my shoulders began to shake.

EIGHT

Leona

EVERYTHING HURT, and someone was crying into my hair. I felt like I was suffering the worst hangover I'd ever had, multiplied tenfold and paired with a vague, generalized sense of impending doom. I was curled in someone's arms—

Kam.

I was curled in *Kam's* arms, and it was his tears slowly soaking my scalp. "*Odama,*" I croaked. Lifting uncoordinated hands, I pawed at him ineffectually—weak as a newborn kitten. His embrace tightened, holding onto me as though he feared I might disappear, but his chest only hitched harder beneath my cheek.

"It's all right, Little One." The basso alpha rumble came from some distance away, and my entire body twitched in unconscious reaction. "Just let him hold you. He tried to explain what was happening earlier, but I think you were too out of it to really understand."

"Understand what?" I rasped, still trying to soothe Kam with hands that didn't want to obey my brain's commands. Everything around me was hazy. Dreamlike. There was something important I should be thinking about, but try as I might, I couldn't grab hold of it.

"You've been taking heat blockers for a long time," said that reassuring alpha voice. "That's made this heat way stronger than it normally would be. Trying to tough it out could be medically dangerous for you. I'm lending you my pheromones, and Kam is lending you a hand... so to speak. We're going to need to do that again in a few hours—possibly sooner. It shouldn't be quite as bad this time, since we know not to leave it too long. Until then, you need to rest."

I wasn't at all sure of the meaning of his words. They seemed important, yet I couldn't seem to focus on them. Except for the last part, anyway. How was I supposed to rest when my packmate was upset?

"No," I protested. "*Kam...*"

He gave a harder shudder against me, and his body stiffened as though he were physically dragging his control together. I could smell the faintest whiff of something sharp and lemony rising from his skin, soured by the tang of grief and fear. I'd... never smelled his scent before. How was it possible that I'd never scented him until now?

His chest expanded with an unsteady breath.

"I'm all right, Leo," he whispered. Clearing his throat, he continued in a stronger tone. "Jax said something nice to me, that's all. You know I don't deal with things like that very well."

Again, I had the feeling that I was missing some deeper meaning. I tried once more to lift a hand to his cheek, only to miss and end up pawing at the side of his neck instead. "You're okay?"

He swallowed hard, his throat bobbing. "'Course I am." A slight pause, then, "Is it all right for me to touch you when you need it, since Jax can't?"

I blinked, not sure why the alpha couldn't touch me. He was nearby—I could smell his heavy, comforting scent. But as for the rest of it…

"You're my pack," I told him, and burrowed a bit closer against his body.

He curled around me. "I didn't hurt you, though?"

I tried to take stock, and decided I'd been right before. "*Everything* hurts," I said.

"That's because we left it too long," said the alpha.

Jax.

The alpha's name was Jax, and that should have been important, though I wasn't sure how, exactly.

"Mmph," I said against Kam's collarbone, my hazy thoughts growing cloudier.

"We won't make that mistake next time," Jax assured me. "The next peak won't be so bad."

Again, I wondered why he was staying so far away. It would be much nicer if he were over here, curled up next to Kam and me. Maybe then, Kam wouldn't cry anymore. The fuzzy gray clouds abruptly smothered me, and I slipped into a doze.

———◆———

I came back to myself—after a fashion, at least—when the aching emptiness inside me yawned wide once more. I *wanted*. My wanting was an endless void that could only be filled by the alpha across the room.

I didn't understand why he wouldn't give me what I needed, no matter how much I begged and cried. Instead, Kam urged me onto my hands and knees as the fever grew, and something filled me that wasn't an alpha's cock. It wasn't what my body yearned for—but it was better than nothing. My pheromones swirled together with the alpha's, eventually triggering a shuddering release of the horrible tension. Again, that faint hint of gingery citrus wafted among the stronger scents choking the room.

Sleep came, followed by something that was almost like wakefulness, but not quite. The alpha said nice things to me in that reassuring, rumbly tone, while Kam held me and stroked my hair. It was pleasant. Time passed. The pattern repeated once more. Afterward, the arms holding me trembled with exhaustion, or maybe something else... something less to do with the physical.

Distantly, I wondered how long this would go on. Something about the thought triggered that same sense of impending doom I'd felt earlier—the one that had been hanging over me for some time now. I mewled, not able to summon words to express my fears.

"Rest, Leona," said the alpha, with a hint of command behind the words. "We'll worry about the next part when it comes."

My body knew what to do with an alpha command, at least. It went boneless, subsiding into sleep.

Some time later, unwelcome scents intruded into my little bubble, setting off alarm bells. *Betas*, my instincts screamed. *Not pack.* At the same instant, the alpha's pheromones spiked with protective aggression.

"Oh, no," Kam said quietly, a world of fear lurking behind the simple words.

The combined signals of *danger, danger* should have snapped me back into something approaching coherence, but I still couldn't seem to control my muscles properly. Adrenaline sloshed around my system with nowhere to go, though it at least expanded my bubble of awareness to encompass the rest of the room I was lying in.

Not a room. A cell.

Parts of the recent past managed to shoehorn their way into my heat-dazed consciousness. Jax had already lunged to his feet, his low growl rolling around the enclosed space as the lock on the heavy cell door clanked open. Kam settled me against the cave wall and knelt in front of me, also facing the door, his arms splayed out to cage my body behind his. He was shaking like a leaf in the wind.

The details were hazy in my memory, but I knew someone was coming for us. When they took us, bad things were going to happen—and I was helpless, barely able to control my own limbs. The door swung open on shrieking hinges, the sound scraping across my nerves like nails on a blackboard. The barrel of a familiar rifle entered first.

Excited voices cut through the air, speaking rapidly with words I couldn't decipher. I peered around Kam's body, my heart thudding. Jax growled again, taking a threatening step toward the guards. The rifle steadied, fixed on him. The other guard pointed a finger toward Kam and me, still talking rapidly. After a moment, both of the men withdrew, and the heavy lock clunked into place, securing the cell door.

"Jax," Kam said, once they'd gone. "Please talk to me. Are you thinking right now, or reacting? Because we're in serious trouble."

The alpha seemed to have grown six inches taller and broader in the space of thirty seconds. My short-circuiting body tingled with need, and if I'd had any kind of muscle control I probably would have stumbled over and tried to climb him like a tree despite the utter inappropriateness of the urge. Meanwhile, in the background, parts of my brain were frantically trying to reboot.

If you try to protect us, they'll just shoot you, I wanted to say, but the words were caught in my throat.

Jax made another low noise of anger. Rather than answer Kam's hesitant question, he turned and strode toward us, moving Kam aside with a gentle hand and scooping me up as though I weighed nothing. He carried me to the wall next to the door, and set me down. The door was designed to open inward, I realized distantly, and it would block me from the immediate view of anyone entering. When I was settled, he herded Kam to huddle next to me. Kam immediately wrapped an arm around my shoulders, holding tight.

Jax crossed the cell, still without a word, and attacked the wooden box that acted as the seat for the latrine, tearing at it with his bare hands. He came up a few moments later with a splintered length of board, wielding it like a club.

"They'll kill you," Kam whispered.

Jax didn't reply. Instead, he returned to the door and positioned himself on the other side from us, makeshift weapon held at the ready.

Heavy footsteps approached—more of them this time.

"Oh, god," Kam said, his fingers clutching the material of my battered blouse.

NINE

Kameron

THE DOOR OPENED again, but only a few inches. It wasn't enough space for Jax to wield his improvised club, or for him to force his way out of the cell. I held Leo close against my side, painfully aware that we had no chance of resisting if the guards got past Jax.

A slender gun barrel poked through the gap—different than the chunky semi-automatic rifle that had greeted us on previous visits. Before I could brace for the inevitable heartbreak to come, the barrel jerked. The retort was strangely quiet, like the sound of a small-caliber pistol with a silencer fitted. Rather than falling down with blood spurting from a gunshot wound, Jax only flinched.

He remained standing, but his hand flew convulsively to his chest, where a fletched dart hung from one bulging pectoral muscle. With a roar, he ripped it free and threw it to the side. Faster than I could follow, he reached out and grabbed the tranquilizer gun, using it to yank the bearer into the door with an ugly clang of flesh against metal.

Dragging the gunman with him, he snarled and staggered through the gap, disappearing into the corridor beyond. I resisted the urge to squeeze my eyes shut as shouts and thumps echoed against the cave walls.

Weak fingers tangled in the material of my shirt.

"Kam," Leo slurred. "Don' resist when they come for me. Let th'm take me. They don' know you're omega. Jus' me."

My stomach churned. She wanted me to hand her over to them…to throw her under the bus in some doomed attempt to save myself.

"Stay here, odama." I removed her hand from my shirt and darted across the cell in search of another usable length of board. The pickings weren't great, but I grabbed a piece that would extend my reach a bit, with the added bonus of a couple of nails sticking out of one end.

Outside, the shouting had subsided in favor of the thumping. I knew better than to hope that meant Jax was winning. They'd tranqed him. As soon as the drugs took him down, we were toast. I hid behind the open door, holding the sad piece of wood like a cricket bat. They might slam the thing open on their way in and squash me against the wall like a bug—but at least they wouldn't see me right away. It was the only chance we had.

The fight in the hallway went ominously quiet. Boots tramped toward the door.

"Kam," Leo said desperately. *"Let them take me."*

Answering her would have given away my position. Not that there were, y'know, too many places to hide inside this bare cell. For the second time in my life, I stood motionless, barely breathing... convinced I was about to die. The footsteps reached the half-open doorway.

I held my breath, waiting. An instant later—with perfect irony—the heavy door rammed into me beneath the force of a heavy shove, sending me staggering even as I tried to dodge out of the way. I tripped over Leo's legs and hit the ground hard. A boot in the ribs drove the remaining air from my lungs, and gray splotches erupted in my vision.

As though underwater, I heard the men exchange another round of rapid-fire Turkish. I tried to roll over and crawl toward them as two of them hefted Leo up by the arms and dragged her away. Uselessly, I patted the packed dirt in search of my pathetic piece of broken wood. Aside from the gasp she'd let out when I stumbled over her body on my ignominious way to the ground, Leo was utterly silent as they hauled her from the cell. I wasn't sure if that was better or worse than if she'd been screaming.

The door slammed unceremoniously shut while I was still scrabbling toward it on my hands and knees. I staggered to my feet and half-fell against it, my palms slapping the un-yielding metal.

The lock clicked with a terrible sense of fi-nality.

My knees gave up on the job of holding me upright, and I crumpled to the floor, my fingernails scraping against the door on the way down. I stared at the rusty metal with un-seeing eyes, a horrible sense of numbness washing over me like frigid, brackish water.

My companions were gone, dragged off to face who-knew-what unimaginable horrors. I had failed them… and now I was alone.

◆

Somehow, I managed to crawl a few feet away, where I at least wouldn't get slammed by the door again, the next time it opened. I had no illusions that our captors had forgotten about me. As a perceived beta weakling who posed no threat, I had simply become a lower priority than an omega in heat.

I remembered this heavy numbness all too well, although I wished I didn't. The feeling of being caged alone, knowing in the depths of my gut that everyone I cared about was either dead or facing the kind of unimaginable tor-ture that only angry betas could devise.

Committee sympathizers had come for my family in Kolkata when I was twelve. We were purebreds—an ancient family line that had been influential in the Bengal region's silk trade since the fifteen hundreds. For centuries, we'd managed to avoid the cyclical tensions between betas and the old, alphomic bloodlines. Strategic bribery... political influence... even disappearing underground for a generation or two, on occasion—these were the things that had allowed my family to endure. To flourish, even.

Perhaps that long history of overcoming the odds had made us complacent. When the end came, I'd still been a pup to all intents and purposes. Naive, trusting, and far too pretty for my own good. In the months leading up to the pogrom, I'd overheard the adults talking in solemn whispers from time to time, but when the vigilantes arrived with guns and shackles, I hadn't truly understood what was about to happen.

The adults had been rounded up and taken to the courtyard. Two men in black, military-style fatigues had held my littermates and me at gunpoint in the grand hall of the old house. I still remembered the sound of gunfire outside; remembered thinking that it must be fireworks, even though it was daylight and there was no festival.

After the courtyard fell silent, a third man came in and checked us over, one by one, verifying our sex. My three alpha brothers and sisters were taken away. I never saw them again. I learned later that alphas were in low demand for the slave trade at the time, since a single alpha could impregnate many omegas.

Of my family, I was the only one with enough potential economic value to make my life worth keeping.

They collared me and dragged me to a truck with a cage in the back. I watched my family home disappear into the distance with almost exactly the same dead feeling that was currently crushing my lungs beneath its weight.

How much time had passed since Leo and Jax had been taken? I wasn't sure. I thought it had only been fifteen minutes or so, but it was entirely possible that my fugue state had distorted my perception of time.

What sort of things could be done to an unconscious alpha and a heat-dazed omega in the space of fifteen minutes? My gorge rose uncontrollably. I staggered onto shaky legs and barely made it to the uncovered latrine hole before losing my stomach contents. Heaving made my bruised ribs feel like they were about to crack in two, but I welcomed the pain. I deserved far worse for not having protected my vulnerable packmate when she needed me.

Muffled gunfire reached me through the walls. My heart stuttered and skipped. I fell back, landing on my ass. Denial raged through me, burning away the comforting numbness.

"No," I whispered... but there was no one left to hear it.

There was... *no one left*.

The gunfire came again—the *rat-a-tat-tat* of a fully automatic rifle answered by the slower retorts of something semi-automatic. I caught my breath, trying to make sense of the sounds. It would only have taken two bullets to finish Leo and Jax. Unless Jax had woken up from the tranquilizer… maybe grabbed a weapon and started fighting back?

But try as I could, I wasn't able to make the scenario fit what I was hearing. He'd been down for the count. Even if he'd regained consciousness, he would have been sluggish and uncoordinated from the drugs.

The weapons fire stopped. I sat frozen on the ground next to the shit pit, the astringent taste of bile coating my throat and tongue.

"*Clear!*" called a distant voice, speaking English.

"*Clear!*" came a different voice, closer this time.

The shuffle of boots moving fast—but with an attempt at stealth—approached my cell door. A face appeared in the small, barred window, silhouetted from behind by the light bulb hanging in the corridor. I still sat unmoving, in plain view. My mouth was hanging open.

"*Target Two located!*" snapped a low, female voice.

A few moments later, the lock clicked and the door swung open. Three figures in dark military garb and balaclavas swarmed into the cell, fanning out to cover every corner of the small space with their weapons. My vision blurred double, images of the day my family was massacred overlaid with images of the present. I still couldn't move—all of my muscles were locked solid with tension.

Cell secured, two of the figures lowered their weapons.

"Shit," said the tallest one. "You can smell that, right?"

The female—the female *alpha*—who'd first peered into the cell gave a sharp nod of confirmation. Then she turned on her heel without a word and went to guard the entrance, weapon held at the ready. Meanwhile, the much shorter and slighter figure on the left lifted his free hand and peeled back his balaclava. I blinked as Rhys Beckett, the beta head of our security team, ran an assessing gaze over me. An ugly, half-healed cut decorated his cheekbone. His expression grew noticeably tight around the eyes as he took in the scene.

"Well," he said, sounding resigned. "This just got a lot more complicated than I'd bargained for."

TEN

Flynn

THE SMELL OF a terrified omega in heat clung to the interior of the cell, making my dick hard at the same time it roused my protective instincts. Beckett wasn't kidding about this mess being a hundred times more complicated than we'd bargained for.

"There are two scents here," Alex threw over her shoulder. "Besides Jax, I mean."

Thoughts of exactly how I'd torture anyone who'd hurt or killed Jax swirled through my head, but I set them aside. I took another breath, letting the fear-tainted perfume in the air settle over the back of my tongue. Alex was right. Not a surprise, since Alex was *always* right about things. That was why she led our pack, after all.

I let my AK-47 drop to hang from its shoulder sling and crossed to Mr. Patel. He didn't look so good. His face was gray and pasty beneath his olive skin, and the sour smell of fresh vomit wafted from the hole in the ground next to him. In that same corner of the cell, someone had torn apart something made of wood. My money was on Jax, trying to arm himself for a fight.

I reached a hand down and hooked Mr. Patel's upper arm, pulling him to his feet. He staggered, half-falling against me, and I took the chance to grab a whiff of the skin at the juncture of his neck and shoulder. He shivered in reaction as I set him back on his feet.

"Omega," I confirmed. "Faint, though."

Beckett shot me a glance. "Flynn, please don't sniff the ambassadorial staff during a rescue mission."

I shrugged. "How else are we supposed to know for sure, boss?"

A haunted look had drawn Mr. Patel's pretty features into haggard lines. That bare hint of lemony perfume told me most of what I needed to know about him. If he'd been on pheromone suppressors that had worn off during his captivity, his perfume would have been at full strength. He must have been one of the ones the betas had caught and mutilated rather than use for breeding. We'd probably only been able to scent him at all because he'd been trapped in a cell with another omega in heat for days on end.

Part of me was impressed, in a distant and detached sort of way. If both he and Ambassador McCready had been hiding in plain sight all this time, they'd done a hell of a good job of it.

"Please," Mr. Patel rasped. "Please… the others. You have to help them."

He was pleading with me directly—not with Beckett. I wondered if he thought we were going to arrest him on the spot for being an unregistered omega. To be fair, that's probably what most people would expect us to do. Or, at least, what they would expect *Beckett* to do.

"That *is* why we're here, Mr. Patel," Beckett said mildly. "To start with, I need you to tell me everything you know. The others' survival could depend on you being completely forthright with me."

Patel blanched further, as though he'd taken Beckett's statement as a thinly veiled threat.

"He didn't mean it that way," I explained. "He just wants you to tell us what happened."

Terrified brown eyes met mine, and that unwanted protective instinct flared. Again, I set it aside. I could see him struggling with himself, every emotion visible on his face. He must have better self-control than this in the normal course of things, I thought, or he would have been found out years ago.

Whatever the case, I saw the moment he decided; saw his last defenses fall. His chin dropped in submission as his eyes slid closed.

"Leona and I are both unregistered omegas," he said hoarsely. "I was sterilized young, but she's still whole. She's been getting by on heat blockers and suppressors. They were hidden in her luggage when we were attacked. She went into heat last night. Jax and I did our best to help her, but she'll be peaking again soon."

"Do you know where she and Jax are being held?" Beckett asked.

Patel shook his head. "Guards tranquilized Jax and dragged both of them away a short time ago."

"How long exactly?" Beckett asked.

Patel squeezed the bridge of his nose with shaking fingers. "I can't be sure. Maybe half an hour?"

Beckett gave a curt nod and motioned for him to continue.

"Yesterday—before Leo's heat came on—they gave us a script to memorize for a video." He glanced around and pointed at a battered notebook lying next to the far wall. "Afterward, they were going to execute us."

I retrieved the notebook and handed it to Beckett, who flipped it open and scanned the contents rapidly. His gaze sharpened.

"What's this about '*a weapon that will eliminate the alphomic threat once and for all*'?" he demanded. "Did they say anything else about this?"

Patel shook his head. "They've barely talked to us. The one who brought us the speech spoke a bit of English. We think they've mostly been speaking Turkish. But you need to go look for the others now. *Please.*"

"Yes," Beckett agreed, stuffing the small notebook into a zippered pocket in his backpack. "We do."

"No signs of life outside," Alex reported, still guarding the door. "Could that really have been all of them?"

We'd only counted eight enemy combatants when we'd stormed in with guns blazing. They were all lying in puddles of their own blood now.

"We'll hope it was, but assume it's not," Beckett said. "Mr. Patel, there's a storage room near the entrance of the cave complex. It will be safer for you to wait for us there than to stay here, on the off chance that there are more terrorists still at large."

The omega's jaw worked. "I should come with—"

"You should stay out of the line of fire and let us do our jobs," Alex interrupted, with the barest hint of an alpha bark behind the words.

Patel's jaw snapped shut, and the muscles in his neck jerked like he had to stop himself from showing throat to us. It should not have been as damned distracting as it was.

"This way. Quickly," Beckett said, and took point. The three of us surrounded our charge and headed for the storage room we'd cleared on the way in.

"There's a scent trail," Alex said. "We may be able to track where they were taken that way."

Beckett gave her a terse nod of acknowledgement. I took Alex's word for it. She had the sharpest nose in the pack, and what was nothing more than a muddle of pheromones to me, might well be more to her.

We left the terrified attaché in the unlocked storage room with orders to stay quiet unless he was discovered, and yell like a banshee if he was. It wasn't ideal, but we'd seen no evidence that any of the terrorists were still here. He would probably be fine, and we couldn't afford to have him unarmed, untrained, and underfoot if we ran into resistance while extracting Jax and the ambassador.

Jax. The annoying bastard had better still be alive. If he was dead, I'd kill him.

"We're following your lead, Alex," Beckett said.

Alex gave a tight nod and led us back to the corridor running in front of the holding cell. We stayed back to avoid further confusing the olfactory landscape, and let her do her thing. Our luck held, in that the place really did seem to be deserted. So far, there'd been no sign of booby traps, either—just rooms full of dusty supplies, makeshift cots, rickety tables with maps piled across them, and lots and lots of rocks.

It was a warren, but it was easy enough to tell which parts were being used and which parts weren't by following the electrical wiring snaking along the walls. We took a couple of wrong turnings and had to backtrack for Alex to pick up the scent again, but eventually even I could smell it like a beacon pointing the way in front of us.

Jax's normal woodsy scent was heavily laden with musk. The omega had gotten to him, and I hoped to hell he'd kept enough of his wits about him to keep from getting dead. Not that I could really blame him too much—that sweet honey and orange blossom perfume was intoxicating as all fuck, and he'd been trapped in an enclosed space with it for god knew how long.

Ahead, the corridor we were traversing ended in a closed door. Like the one on the holding cell, it had a barred window at head height. Beckett stood to one side, poised to open it, and counted us down silently with his fingers.

Three... two... one... *go.*

We swept inside in well-practiced choreography, accommodating the lack of our fourth as effectively as possible. I swung my AK-47 around in a smooth arc, clearing my quadrant of the room. The others did the same, ranging out to check any possible hiding place.

It was empty except for two figures lying unmoving on bare medical tables. In the absence of active threats, I lowered my weapon and let myself look at them properly.

Alex cursed, short and sharp.

Jax was out cold, though a heart monitor on a cart next to him beeped out a slow, steady rhythm. An IV bag hung above the table, dripping fluid through a tube attached to his arm. Alex was at his side in two strides, pulling the needle out. I watched him long enough to confirm the rise and fall of his chest before my gaze was drawn to the second figure like iron filings to a magnet. Leona McCready's heat-scent slammed into me like a freight train, knocking every single thought from my head except one.

Mate.

Her long red hair was sweat-soaked, and her skin was pale except for two feverish spots of color on her cheekbones. *Jesus Christ*—her skirt was stained in front where she'd dripped slick onto it—presumably while she was on her hands and knees, presenting for sex.

The mental image felt like a bomb going off in my brain. In the space between one heartbeat and the next, I knew that both of these omegas were meant to be ours. A figure approached her, and a growl rumbled up from my chest. I took a step toward the medical table without consciously deciding to move.

"*Flynn!*" There was nothing subdued about Alex's alpha bark this time. It slapped my instincts upside the head, and I froze, blinking.

The figure standing near the ambassador resolved into Beckett. He was watching me closely, though without a hint of fear.

"Come help me with her," he said, ignoring the fact that I'd just snarled at him.

I strode to the table and looked down at the battered porcelain doll lying there.

"I'm reasonably sure she's been sedated as well," Beckett said. "Not a bad thing under the circumstances, assuming they used something safe. Take her pulse and count her respirations for me while I help Alex with Jax. Then you're going to need to carry him out of here. Alex can take the ambassador."

I could do that. With a nod of acknowledgement, I took the excuse I'd been given to lift one delicate wrist. My hand dwarfed it. I was only vaguely aware of Beckett stowing the IV bag of whatever they'd been pumping into Jax's veins inside his pack. Then, he and Alex efficiently disconnected the heart monitor leads from Jax's chest.

"Pulse and respiration's depressed, but not dangerously so," I reported, not immediately letting go of Ambassador McCready's wrist.

"Good," Beckett said tersely. He started rummaging through a mini-fridge in the corner of the makeshift lab, checking labels. A few moments later, he straightened with a couple of vials in his hand. The vials and a handful of syringes joined the IV bag already stashed in his pack.

The creamy skin beneath my fingertips felt too warm, making me think the ambassador's body was trying to climb toward its next heat-peak despite her unconscious state. A tiny whimper slipped past her full lips, and in that moment I would have thrown down with Alex for dibs on carrying her, despite Beckett's orders.

That was stupid, though. While Alex could probably lift Jax into a fireman's carry if circumstances required it, his weight would interfere with her ability to move fast and use a weapon much more than it would with mine. My instincts grumbled in discontent, but I lowered the ambassador's arm gently to the table and turned to the others.

"Ready?" I asked.

"Yes," Beckett said, grim-faced. "Let's collect Mr. Patel so we can get the hell out of here. And, please god, let the safehouse our contact arranged for us be as safe as it's cracked up to be."

"This is turning into ten different kinds of clusterfuck," Alex said, equally grim.

She hauled the ambassador's body into a sitting position and ducked under her torso, distributing the omega's negligible weight across her shoulders as she straightened. I had no idea how she managed to avoid sniffing Leona McCready's skin like a cocaine addict snorting a fresh line—but then again, Alex hadn't earned the nickname *The Ice Queen* for nothing.

I crossed to Jax and hauled him up the same way, the two cracked ribs I'd sustained in the I.E.D. attack grinding painfully as I steadied the bastard's bulk. Securing him in the fireman's carry with my left arm around his thigh, I grasped my weapon right-handed and brought it into firing position.

Beckett had completed one final sweep of the lab, gathering up a few papers that had been left behind and shoving them into his pack with everything else. "Move out," he ordered. "Stay sharp—I'll take point. Let's get these three to safety, and hope like hell there's a medical lab somewhere around here that's equipped to figure out what they were pumping into Jax."

"Your lips to god's ears," Alex muttered, and fell into step next to me.

ELEVEN

Kameron

THE DARK storage room might have been even worse than the cell. I crouched among a pile of crates in the corner, trying to convince myself that Leo and Jax were still alive... that Beckett wouldn't arrest us and turn us over to the Committee the moment he got his alpha away safely.

Time was still moving oddly. My bruised side ached and throbbed in sync with my heartbeat. I had no idea how long it was likely to take to find the others. And what if they were still being guarded? What if Beckett's team fell to a counterattack in some deep part of the cave complex where I wouldn't hear the gunfire?

A sharp rap sounded against the door, and I nearly jumped out of my skin. I rose on shaky legs, keeping to the shadowed corner as the knob turned and the door creaked open.

"We're leaving," Beckett said.

"The others?" I asked breathlessly.

"We've got them. Move." He jerked his chin toward the corridor, all business.

He would have said something if they were dead, I told myself firmly. He'd be acting more upset. More… *something*.

Outside, the huge, dark-skinned alpha— *Flynn?*—had Jax's limp body slung over his shoulders. The female alpha, Alex, had Leo draped over her shoulders in the same way. The air caught in my lungs.

"Are they—" The words burst free without conscious intent.

"Alive," Alex confirmed. As if to drive home the point, Leo gave a low moan.

"Time isn't really on our side here," Beckett said.

I broke free of my paralysis, following the others out of the cave system. It was cloudy outside, which was probably just as well. Even this dreary gray light was enough to hurt my eyes after days spent trapped in the shadows. How long had it been since I'd seen the sky? I couldn't have said what day of the week it was. More worryingly, I couldn't have said what day it had been when we were first taken.

"It's some distance to our transportation, I'm sorry to say." Beckett kept his voice low. He raked an assessing gaze over me, as though trying to decide if I was going to slow them down. Then his pale eyes scanned the crags and peaks around us.

Did he expect an attack? More terrorists lying in wait for an ambush? The hair on the back of my neck prickled. The skin between my shoulder blades felt tight and vulnerable.

No gunfire erupted as we made our way down a rocky slope toward a wooded canyon. I would scarcely have credited the alphas' ability to negotiate the poor footing with the weight of their unconscious burdens—especially while also holding their bulky automatic weapons at the ready.

After a few minutes without any further drama ensuing, we reached the relative cover of a large pile of boulders. Beckett drew a water bottle and an energy bar out of his pack, handing both items to me wordlessly. I opened the water with relief, rinsing my mouth and spitting before drinking half of it in one go. The energy bar, I stuffed into my trouser pocket—not at all sure my stomach could handle it right now.

"This isn't right," I said, careful to keep my voice low, as Beckett had done. "When they dragged us into the caves, it was only a short distance from where they'd parked the vehicles. They had bags over our heads, but I'm sure there was a road near the cave entrance. Or a track, at least."

Beckett's eyes didn't stray from their careful observation of our surroundings. "I'm willing to bet there's a second exit from the cave system. For one thing, we rescued the other two from some kind of lab, and none of the men we killed on our way in looked like either scientists or medical personnel."

"You think there were other people there, and they got away?" I asked, not liking the potential ramifications of that idea *at all*.

"It seems likely," Beckett said.

We started down a particularly steep slope, scree rolling beneath my feet like jagged marbles, and I had to focus on keeping my rubbery legs steady enough not to fall. Eventually, the landscape evened out into what must have been a dry riverbed. I could see a Range Rover, or some similarly shaped off-road vehicle, parked in the distance.

Somehow, I made it the rest of the way without collapsing or significantly slowing the others down—though my vision was tunneling in, gray fog creeping around the edges by the time we finally arrived.

"Put Jax in the back," Beckett said. "Check his vitals again and make sure he's in the recovery position. Alex, you're driving. Flynn, you're riding shotgun."

After a brief flurry of activity, I found myself in the back seat, propping Leo upright as Beckett climbed in on her other side and slammed the door. The engine rumbled to life. A moment later we were moving—heading, presumably, for civilization, where Leo would still be in heat and our secret would be well and truly out.

Leo squirmed against me, panting. Her eyes had opened to slits, but she didn't seem truly aware of what was happening. Beckett rummaged in the black backpack he'd slung onto the floorboard between his feet and came up with a vial and a syringe.

"What are you doing?" I asked in alarm.

"She was sedated when we found her," he said. "Under the circumstances, I think that's not a bad plan."

Flynn snorted. "Unless you want this pile of bolts to end up wrapped around a tree, it probably is a good plan, yeah."

"Oh, ye of little faith," Alex muttered from the driver's seat.

"It won't work forever," Beckett said. "Not in her current condition. But we're a good couple of hours out from our temporary safehouse, and I'd rather not make that kind of drive with an omega climbing a heat-peak and two alphas in the front seat."

I digested that, steadying Leo against a particularly violent lurch as the vehicle juddered over the uneven terrain.

"All right," I said slowly — not that I was in any position to object. "If you're sure it's safe for her. Next question. Are we under arrest?"

"No," Beckett replied without hesitation.

I wanted to press the issue further. I *should* have pressed it further. There was too much here that wasn't adding up. Why wasn't Jax — allegedly a subjugated alpha — chemically castrated? How had a civilian government security team managed to get resources for a specialist anti-terrorist military extraction mission in a matter of days? And… a *safehouse*? In a foreign country?

The answers to these questions were important. It wasn't an exaggeration to say that our lives might well depend on them. Placing us under immediate arrest before dragging us to the nearest embassy for processing and extradition to the Committee would absolutely have been the correct protocol under these circumstances. The concept of diplomatic immunity in international law was still on the books, but only for betas. It hadn't applied to alphas or omegas for decades now.

And yet, all I could do was cling to Leo's arm, breathing deeply to keep my churning stomach contents in place and hold the swirling gray mist at the edges of my vision at bay. Beckett drew the contents of the tiny glass vial into the syringe with steady hands despite the jouncing of the vehicle. When Leo's perfume thickened, her eyes growing more aware and her movements more purposeful, he called for a halt long enough to sedate her again.

I spared a worried thought for Jax, curled on his side in the back. He was tough. I knew the others were banking on the extreme measures that were usually required to kill an alpha. Realistically, without knowing what had been done to him—and in the absence of medical equipment—there wasn't anything to be done except getting him someplace safe for medical attention.

Before long, Leo lapsed into unconsciousness again, though her perfume still filled the interior of the Rover. After what seemed like forever, Alex pulled onto an honest-to-god road, and the ride smoothed out. I lapsed into a sort of fugue state; my brain having evidently decided that it was throwing in the towel for a bit.

Despite open windows and the sedative's best efforts, the inside of the vehicle was a miasma of pheromones. Spicy cardamom—that was Flynn. Rich jasmine and sandalwood—that had to be Alex. Jax's now-familiar ambergris and cypress was muted, soured by whatever our kidnappers had done to him. Leo's sweet scent overpowered them all. I couldn't get a thing off Beckett except the chemical smell of underarm deodorant—the kind that so many betas seemed to favor.

Just sit back and let the nice alphas take care of everything, my instincts tried to tell me, despite how disastrous that had the potential to be. I couldn't give into omega weakness—I was currently the only thing standing between Leo and whatever was coming next.

My silent internal battle raged. The practical upshot was that I ended up being totally useless, my thoughts locked in an ever-tightening spiral of stress and fear. When the vehicle turned onto what appeared to be a private drive, it came as a complete surprise. I had no idea how long I'd been staring into nothing, clutching Leo's arm like a lifeline.

"This is it," Beckett said dryly, as a cabin came into view through the trees. "Apparently."

"Utilities?" Alex asked. "Food?"

"Allegedly," Beckett replied.

Alex pulled the Range Rover up to the front door and parked it.

"Why have you brought us here?" I asked, fresh dread bubbling up at the realization of how remote this place appeared to be.

"Because no one will think to come looking for you here, while we figure out what the hell's going on with this so-called Beta Liberation Front," Beckett said. "The fact that there's no one else living close enough to smell an omega in heat is a happy bonus. Stay here."

He opened the door and got out, closing it behind him. Pistol in hand, he disappeared around the side of the cabin and returned after a few moments, evidently with a key. The rest of us waited in awkward silence as he went inside. A couple of minutes later, he returned. Flynn stuck his head out of the passenger-side window, and Beckett leaned against the door to speak with him.

"There's water and electricity," he reported, "along with enough shelf-stable food in the pantry to last about a week, which is longer than we'll need. One of you needs to stay here while we get Jax medical attention and start investigating this alleged terrorist weapon. Alex, it's your call who stays and who goes."

The female alpha's catlike green eyes flicked back to meet mine via the medium of the rearview mirror for the barest of instants. Then she turned her attention to Flynn, pinning his gaze.

"You're on omega duty," she said. "And since you're also our resident pervert, I'm hoping you've got something stashed in your luggage that will help her?"

Flynn shrugged. "Yeah, probably."

"Good," Alex said. "Now give me your word you won't cross any boundaries. Whatever the omegas say goes, and it doesn't count if it's not proper consent."

"I know," Flynn replied. "I promise, *alef.* I'll watch over them while you're gone."

"Let's get them inside," Beckett said, backing away from the passenger door to let the huge alpha get out.

Flynn gestured toward the back of the Range Rover. "Someone strip off Jax's shirt and bring it inside. It stinks like him, so it'll help." He opened the door on my side and leaned in. "Can you make it inside on your own, Mr. Patel?"

The rational part of my mind still wasn't sold on the wisdom of going into this remote cabin with my unconscious packmate and an alpha I barely knew. The part that was running on fumes ensured that I nodded wordlessly and climbed out, bracing myself on unsteady legs. Beckett was at the back of the vehicle, fussing over Jax. I wanted to check on the blond alpha… maybe thank him, even though he probably wouldn't be able to hear it.

I didn't move. *Couldn't* move.

Flynn disappeared from my side for a moment and returned to shove a filthy under-shirt into my hands. I stared at it cluelessly as Jax's scent floated to my nostrils. The dark-skinned alpha leaned into the back seat and scooped Leo into his arms, pausing for a sec-ond to sniff deeply at the base of her neck — just as he'd done to me earlier.

I let myself be herded into the cabin, tak-ing in the smell of dust and neglect. Beckett came inside just long enough to drop a couple of duffel bags by the door.

"I'll send Alex back with the Range Rover as soon as we get Jax the care he needs." He wrapped his fingers around Flynn's massive bicep in a gesture that seemed almost paternal. "You'll be safe here in the meantime, and so will they."

"Course we will, boss." Flynn looked down at the unconscious burden in his arms. "Told you. I'll take care of them."

Beckett gave him a tight smile. "I know you will, Flynn." His pale, sea-foam colored eyes met mine. "Mr. Patel, I know this is ask-ing a lot of your trust — but everything will be all right. No one will harm you here."

All I could manage was a tense nod. Any-thing else would have given away how badly I was trembling. I wanted so desperately to be-lieve it… but I couldn't ignore the clamoring of my shattered nerves. Right now, it didn't feel like *anything* would be all right—not ever again.

Beckett gave Flynn a final firm pat on the shoulder and left, ready to rush his injured alpha back to civilization. I should have demanded to know where, exactly, we were. Would Alex and Beckett be driving to a hospital in Târgovişte? Were we anyplace *near* Târgovişte anymore? Instead, I stared blankly at Flynn.

He stared back. "You're about to fall over, I think."

Was I?

Oh… right. I totally was.

"Yes," I whispered. "Sorry."

He tilted a massive bicep toward me. "Grab an arm, then. Let's see if we can get you both cleaned up and fed before this one wakes up and needs attention."

I grabbed the arm and held on.

The interior of the cabin was an undifferentiated blur as Flynn led me deeper into the structure. I blinked as an overhead light fixture flared into life, revealing a bathroom. It was basic—almost institutional—with a sink, a toilet, and an area ringed off by a plastic shower curtain. The floor was tile, sloping subtly toward the shower area at the back. A set of plain shelves near the sink held folded towels.

Flynn lowered Leo onto the closed toilet seat and steadied her in a seated position, her chin lolling against her chest. "She's asleep, so you have to tell me what's a boundary and what isn't. Can I bathe her?"

I dragged as many brain cells back into working order as I could. "Uh... no. I'll do it."

"Okay," he said. "I can lift her in for you, though? Maybe keep her underwear on if that would make you feel safer."

I nodded, aware that I'd already made too many compromises on my packmate's behalf—and there would probably be more to come. "All right," I told him.

Flynn nodded and efficiently stripped off the filthy remains of Leo's smart gray skirtsuit, leaving her in her light green bra and panties. He sniffed her again, and I tried not to bristle.

"Don't think we have all that long," he said, lifting her and carrying her across the room to the shower area. He placed her carefully on the floor, back propped in the corner. "Get in there with her. There's soap, and I'll bring you the shampoo I stole from the hotel room in Bucharest."

Numbly, I stripped off my clothes, too wrecked to have any concern for my nakedness. It didn't matter—my scarred and abused body hadn't felt like *me* for a very long time. Flynn's deep brown eyes raked down my length, and I shivered under his gaze.

"Back in a minute with the shampoo," he said.

I stepped into the shower and turned on the water, angling the spray away from Leo's body. It ran rusty for a few seconds before clearing, and warmed up a few seconds after that. A large hand passed a small shampoo bottle around the edge of the plastic curtain, and I took it.

"I'm gonna go get things ready for you," Flynn said, over the sound of spattering water drops. "Don't either of you drown while I'm gone, or I'll be pissed."

I still couldn't seem to muster words. Flynn left to do… whatever the hell he was doing, and I made a concerted attempt to scrub the worst of the last few days off both of us. Leo woke as I was trying to wrestle her around to get her hair rinsed properly.

"Kam?" she slurred. "What's going on?"

"It's all right. We're safe, I think. I'm getting us cleaned up," I answered, aware that my voice sounded flat and distant. "Lean your head back for me."

Her head lolled backward into the spray, and a sensual groan of pleasure cut through the steamy atmosphere. When I was confident I'd managed to rinse most of the soap off of both of us, I turned off the shower and retrieved a couple of towels.

Drying off was hit or miss, and it was fairly apparent the pale bra and panties weren't doing much for Leo's modesty while they were damp. I wrapped the towel around her as best I could, and was contemplating my own filthy clothes when Flynn returned.

He stopped in the doorway, blinking, and I couldn't miss the way his brown eyes darkened. After a beat, he broke himself free of his temporary paralysis. "Damn, but if that isn't a sight," he muttered, seemingly to himself. He shoved a bundle of cloth at me, and I took it. "Here. T-shirt and boxers. Figured you wouldn't be in a hurry to dress in what you've been wearing."

"Thank you," I managed, and shrugged into the comically oversized clothing. It smelled like laundry detergent, with only the faintest clinging scent of spicy musk.

"Brought one for her, too. Just the shirt, though. It's not clean—thought the smell might help her some, later." Flynn hesitated. "Jax's would be better, but it's pretty disgusting with all the blood and stuff on it. I figure we can just put it in the nest for her in case she wants it."

I stared at him, uncomprehending. The... *nest?*

Blinking free of my confusion, I held my hand out for the other shirt. "She's awake—sort of. I'll help her get this on. Thanks."

He handed it over, and I ducked behind the shower curtain, where Leo was still huddled on the floor in her towel.

"Hey, *odama*," I said, trying to keep my tone soothing. "Smell this for me, and let me know if you want to wear it."

I lifted the soft T-shirt to her nose. She breathed in, and her pupils dilated as she let out a decadent moan.

"That's good enough for me, I guess," I said. "You want to lose the bra first?"

"God yes," she murmured, plucking at it ineffectually.

I helped her out of the bra and into the shirt, which hung on her tiny frame, covering her to mid-thigh. Distantly, I was aware that my desire to fuss over her was pretty much the only thing keeping me on my feet. My stomach—settled somewhat now that I wasn't in imminent fear of death—grumbled, demanding food. I had a sneaking suspicion that my blood sugar levels were sloshing down around my ankles somewhere.

Tossing the damp towel aside, I slid the shower curtain back.

"Hi, Madam Ambassador," Flynn said. "Can I pick you up? I'm supposed to ask first whenever you're awake, but it's going to be hard to move you otherwise."

Unfortunately, Leo's eyes went dazed and overwhelmed the moment they settled on the towering alpha in front of her.

"It's fine," I said quickly. "Let's just get her someplace warm and quiet, please."

Flynn nodded and scooped Leo up as though she weighed nothing. He didn't scent her this time—possibly because her perfume was starting to overwhelm the room's atmosphere again. I followed them out, keeping one hand on the wall for balance.

Flynn nudged an interior door open with his hip and disappeared inside. I slipped in after him to find him laying Leo in the center of a huge pile of pillows, couch cushions, and displaced mattresses in the center of what was probably a bedroom. My jaw dropped open as I scanned the dim, red-lit surroundings. The alpha had pushed all of the furniture to the edges of the room, and draped a sheer, red curtain over the single lampshade. I had no doubt that every bed, couch and chair in the place had been ransacked to construct the makeshift nest, which also boasted several blankets.

Leo groaned in relief and burrowed into the softness.

The room smelled partly of alpha and partly of strangers. The woodsy scent from Jax's blood and sweat-stained undershirt was definitely in the mix. There was something else, as well… something that made my stomach rumble. *Tomato soup?*

"Soup and cheesy crackers are on the side table, Mr. Patel," Flynn said, as though it wasn't remotely unusual that he'd whipped up a heat-nest and also made soup for me in the space of barely half an hour. "She won't eat until the heat breaks, but I expect you're probably going to need it."

TWELVE

Leona

I WAS PRETTY sure this was a dream. And if it was? I'd totally take it. Hard-packed bare dirt had given way to soft pillows and cushions. Frightening shadows had been replaced with a warm, comforting red glow. Except for the hint of stranger-smell clinging to the bedding, it was all reassuringly womb-like.

Nest. My instincts sighed in relief.

Unfortunately, while my instincts might be happier now, my body felt like complete crap. Someone had put me through a meat grinder and topped it off by stuffing my mouth with cotton wool... or possibly with a small, furry animal that had died of gangrene.

One or the other.

I'd regained consciousness in a shower, and Kam had been with me. So had an alpha, but a different one. His pumpkin-spice scent clung to the shirt I was wearing, and that part was okay. I wanted Jax to be here, too—but there was only a stale hint of his scent that smelled...off, somehow. Sick, maybe, or hurt.

Something had happened, and I wasn't clear what it was. Kam and the new alpha spoke to me, but the sense of the words drifted in and out. Mostly *out*, if I was being honest. I was feeling feverish and empty again. Restless, I writhed against the cushions and blankets, trying to transfer more of my scent to them.

"She's getting close," said the new alpha. "I brought something to help. What were you using before to knot her?"

Kam knelt next to me, smelling of… tomatoes? Which seemed really random, somehow. Maybe this was a dream after all.

"My fingers," he said.

"Yeah, this'll be better. Here." A pause, as Kam stretched out an arm, reaching for something.

"Do I want to know why you have a knotting dildo in your luggage?" Kam asked.

"Some beta women like 'em," said the other voice. "Especially when the real thing's too big."

I felt Kam take a breath as though to speak, only to let it out again. "You know what? Never mind." A rubbery-looking cylinder with a bulge at the base entered my field of view. It was a pretty, candy cane shade of spiraling red and white. "Leo, this will be better than my fingers. Can I use this on you?"

I didn't want a candy cane. I wanted the alpha. Too bad my words were gone again. I whimpered in frustration.

"She can't answer," said the alpha. "You have to choose for her. What are my boundaries, Mr. Patel? Can I be in the nest with you?"

Another pause.

"Y-yes. I think it might help. But... keep me between the two of you. And keep your clothes on. Well, except when you need to, you know..."

"Get myself off," the alpha finished for him. "Yeah, okay. Can I talk to you while I'm in the nest?"

"Yes, of course you can talk," Kam said quickly. "Look, I know this whole thing is awful. I'm really sorry about all of this."

The cushions shifted as a heavy weight lowered onto them. The spicy smell of horny alpha grew stronger, and I sucked it in like a drowning woman surfacing for air.

"Why are you sorry?" asked the alpha. "Did you cause any of this?"

"No," Kam said. "But I'm still sorry."

I peered past Kam's slender body as the alpha settled his long, muscular form into the softness of the nest. Saliva pooled in my mouth, and I swallowed hard to keep from drooling.

"You shouldn't be, though," the alpha said. "I'm never sorry—not for anything. Simpler that way."

"I imagine it would be, at that," Kam replied.

"So, you two—you're together? Pack?"

Kam's hand smoothed damp hair away from my face. He was shaking. I leaned into the touch, trying to convey reassurance. "Yes," he said softly.

"That's good," said the alpha. "You hear that, Ambassador? Your *odama*'s going to help you out now. You're ready for him, right?"

There was a question in there, along with a promise of something—even if the details were beyond me at the moment. I rubbed my thighs together, feeling a fresh pulse of slick gathering.

"Like I told Jax, I think we're probably into first name territory at this point," Kam said. "Call me Kam, and she's Leona."

"Sure thing, Kam. I'm still Flynn, though. I've only got the one name." The alpha shifted, his lovely dark eyes stroking over me like liquid heat. "You ready to get warmed up, Leona? Kam could make you come a couple of times—get you all nice and ready for this pretty little silicone cock."

Some of that made it through the fuzz surrounding my brain, and he might as well have poured lava on me. I whined and panted, trying to wriggle out of my soaked panties with uncoordinated movements.

"I don't know if that's—" Kam began, trailing off uncertainly.

There was a pause. "Don't know if that's what?" The alpha rolled onto an elbow. "She's okay with you touching her, right? You were already together."

"Well, yes, but…"

"Then here's the thing, Kam. This heat is going to be miserable for her, and the only relief she's going to get is when she's being sexually satisfied. I wish I could do it, but like I said, I'm not allowed."

I reached across Kam's body and managed to get a weak grip on the alpha's wrist, hoping to pull him toward me. He made a low noise of regret before peeling my fingers loose and lifting my knuckles to his lips, pressing a kiss there. Then he gently set my arm back on Kam's other side.

"It just seems wrong when she's like this," Kam said miserably.

"If you were an alpha, though," he began. "If you could help her through this on your own, and you didn't have to worry about pups or any of the rest of it... you wouldn't just put her on her hands and knees and stick it in her, would you? 'Cause you don't really seem like that kind of person."

Kam took in a shuddering breath. "No, of course I wouldn't."

"Well, we're safe here," the alpha said. "And I promised Alex I'd be good, so you don't have to worry about me. You might as well be nice to her and make this as easy for her as it's going to get. I'll just sit here and enjoy the show until you're ready for me to bust a nut and lend her some pheromones."

Kam let out an odd, rusty-gate-hinge noise that might conceivably have been a hysterical bark of laughter. "God, I must be going insane." The words were as shaky as his hand had been. "Leo, my dearest love, I hope this is the right thing. And I wish I *was* that imaginary alpha, so we could be together properly."

His gentle touch traced my cheek, down my neck to play over the inflamed skin covering my mating gland. I arched and moaned breathlessly, drinking in the tingles of pleasure.

"You two are together exactly as you're meant to be," said the alpha. "You're already perfect; you just need a better world to live in. Now, Kam... touch those beautiful breasts for me, since I can't do it. Fuck—if I could, I'd put my mouth all over every square inch of both of you until the pair of you were screaming for me."

Kam let out another shaky noise and lay down, spooning me from behind in the soft warmth of the nest. "*God*," he said again.

A hand cupped my left breast, and I pressed into the contact like a cat. My nipples hardened, a jolt of sensation spreading downward and releasing a fresh trickle of slick. Lips closed over the tendon in my neck, teeth scraping lightly. I rolled my head to the side, exposing my throat and breathing in spicy alpha musk as it grew heavier in the air.

Pleasure rolled along my nerves, everything so different in this cozy place of safety than it had felt in that horrible bare cave. The painful exhaustion and fear that had been plaguing me fell away, subsumed beneath the feeling of loving hands touching all the places that ached to be touched. A low, rumbling voice narrated a never-ending litany of filthy suggestions interspersed with praise.

Kam's hand drifted down to my sex, stroking through the silken slickness there. It *never* felt like this normally—like there was a spring inside me tightening with every pass of fingers over my nub. He dipped inside my passage, my muscles clenching to try and keep him there. After an endless upward spiral that might have lasted minutes or hours, Kam's tongue rasped over my mating gland and I keened, ecstasy crashing over me.

Kam wrapped his slender body around me and held me as I came down, his arms tight around me. A hint of lemon and ginger tickled my nose beneath Flynn's heavier perfume and my own thick sweetness.

"Jesus H. Christ on a popsicle stick, that was hot," said the alpha. He let out a deep breath. "You're about to peak on us, aren't you, sweet thing? That's okay—Kam's gonna fill you up now. He'll fuck you nice and slow for me. Kam, don't let her have the knot until I say so."

I was still lying on my side, but as the word 'knot' registered, I scrambled inelegantly into position, my lower back arching.

"*Fuck me blind,*" Flynn muttered, like a curse. I heard the rasp of a zipper sliding open.

"I'm here, Leo," Kam said hoarsely. "We've got you, *odama*."

Fingers stroked up and down the length my spine, lighting every nerve through the soft cotton of the pheromone-laden T-shirt. I mewled in approval as something hard and blunt-tipped slid up and down along my labia a few times before entering me.

God, this was so much better than before. It still wasn't exactly what my body wanted, but it was *pleasure, pleasure, pleasure* tingling along my arms and legs, spreading warmth outward from my center. I rocked back and forth shamelessly, trying to get all of it inside me—wallowing in the thickening scent of musk as the alpha chased his own pleasure, barely more than an arm's length away from me.

"Not yet, sweet thing," he said, a low growl lurking beneath the words. "You'll take this knot when I say so, and not before."

"*Good god*," Kam muttered, sounding like he was in danger of fainting. "Alex wasn't kidding about you being the pervert, was she?"

"At least that didn't sound like a complaint," Flynn pointed out, still in that gravelly voice.

I craned around, omega flexibility allowing me to get a glimpse of him fisting that thick alpha cock of his, in time with the slow thrusts making my toes curl. I dragged my eyes up the length of his body until out gazes locked. With a deep groan, he sped his movements and curled forward. Pearly white pulsed and spilled from his dick, coating his hand and stomach.

"Now," he said. "Give it to her now."

"*Jesus*," Kam said, the word emerging awestruck.

The fake cock pressed all the way into me, my entrance stretching to accommodate the thickened knot near the base and then clamping around it. I let out a shriek and climaxed again, squeezing the unyielding length with rhythmic pulses—perfectly and deliciously filled.

Our mingled perfume drove away the lingering scent of the room's previous nameless occupants. Sugar and spice, citrus and ginger.

"You both did so well," Flynn said. "Time to rest now."

The approval in the alpha's voice washed over me like a salve.

As before, Kam helped me roll onto my side. As before, when he pressed against me, he was shaking. My mind felt a tiny bit clearer than it had before. There was no way I could relax into this relative peace when my packmate was barely holding himself together. I squirmed around in his arms until I could peer over his shoulder and meet Flynn's eyes again, biting my lower lip as the toy shifted inside me.

"Alpha?" I asked.

"What is it, sweet thing?" His voice was dark velvet.

"Kam needs you now, but he's afraid to ask."

Next to me, Kam went very still.

"Is that true, Kam?" Flynn asked. "Do you… need me to look after you for a bit?"

Kam took a tiny, hitching breath, and then another. The silence grew heavy.

"Yes, please, alpha," he whispered, after a long, hesitant pause. Another tremor shuddered through his body. "I just… need… something to make all of this go away for a bit."

A low purr rumbled up from Flynn's chest. His weight shifted among the pillows and cushions. Muscular arms closed around Kam from behind.

"Come here, ginger tea," he said. Still purring, the alpha curled his muscular body around my packmate. I squeezed myself against Kam's front, tucking my head under his chin and wrapping my arms around him, too.

"I love you, *odama*," I murmured against Kam's collarbone. I might've been awash in post-orgasmic hormones, but it was still the truth.

"Hear that?" Flynn asked. "Your packmate loves you. It's all right—you're safe now. You're both safe."

Kam held himself with brittle stillness for long moments, his heart pounding a frantic, staccato rhythm against my cheek. Finally, a silent sob jerked free of his chest, followed by another, and another. Flynn curled tighter against him, his big hand coming to rest on my

shoulder as we pressed Kam between us, giving him a safe place to fall apart.

THIRTEEN

Flynn

SOCIAL CUES were complicated, especially in the beta world. That's why I'd always found it easier to trust Alex, or in a pinch, Jax, to make decisions about that kind of stuff, and just do whatever they said. Omegas were easy to understand, though—especially when heat was involved.

Kam was one badly broken omega, partly because beta assholes had apparently gotten hold of him young... but partly because he'd crammed himself into a box that didn't fit. I had a sneaking suspicion that the ambassador—*Leona*—was in pretty much the same spot, though it wouldn't surprise me if she buried the sharp edges a little deeper.

Passing in beta society was hard enough when you were aligned, with your gender matching what they expected of your biological sex. It was even harder if you were unaligned, as everyone in my little pack had ample cause to know. The idea that female alphas and male omegas even existed in the first place seemed to enrage betas. I could only imagine how Kam had twisted himself to fit into the role of *beta male*. Testosterone injections, almost certainly. Brutal gym workouts to maintain the sort of musculature that betas expected, probably.

Meanwhile, Leona would have needed to fight not only the perception that a hyper-feminine woman wasn't suited to a high-stress political post helping to shape international policy, but also the added softness that came with being an omega. Instead of letting it define her, she'd channeled that soft aura into diplomacy, subtly turning an omega's social influence within the pack against hardened beta diplomats and world leaders. How many of them had found themselves talked around to her point of view with no idea how it had happened, I wondered?

The two of them were pack to each other, but it was clear enough they'd never had anyone to guard their nest so they could let down their defenses every once in a while. Kam was trying to play alpha even though he had no bark or bite to back it up—convinced it was his responsibility to protect Leona when she was at her most vulnerable. No wonder he was shaking apart in the circle of my arms, clinging to his *odama* as he cried out the stress and terror of the past several days.

When it came to emotion, I didn't feel all that much in the normal course of things—and that was the way I liked it. *Numb*. When I did get hit with feelings, it was simple stuff. I was angry at whoever had hurt Jax. If the stuck-up bastard ended up dying on us, I'd be angry at him, too. The emotions of the heat-nest were straightforward, even if I'd only experienced them firsthand on a tiny number of occasions. I hadn't been a breeder on the slave plantation—except once, when a high-value omega was cycling and they didn't have any better options to get her pupped on schedule. Mostly, though, I'd just been muscle. A laborer.

But an alpha still knew what was needed. Protectiveness. Steadiness. That was what we provided, when omegas were vulnerable and coming apart at the seams. It was probably the same thing that made beta women flock to us, whenever they thought they could get away with it without being shamed.

I shifted in the nest of pillows. My dick ached—my knot wishing it was in a nice warm passage where it wanted to be. Of course, my dick ached a lot after sex, since just because beta women thought they could take the alpha knot, it didn't mean splitting them open with *my* knot was something that would end well. Hence the more reasonably sized dildo, among other handy contraband sex toys.

At least it had come in useful here. From her reaction to the modest, beta-sized toy, it was pretty clear Leona was a virgin. I wondered if Kam had ever let an alpha try to work around whatever had been done to his body when they sterilized him. I'd been with two other sterilized omegas sexually since I'd been drafted into the UFNA military program. One had still been able to get off with a bit of patience and creativity. One hadn't.

I vowed to find out which camp Kam fell into the next time Leona went into heat—because, to my mind, there was no question that both of them would be ours by then. I could picture it with total clarity inside my head. Jax would recover from whatever shit the terrorists had pumped into him. Kam and Leona would accept our courting and agree to mate with us. Three months from now, we'd take turns knotting Leona through her peaks. Well... okay. Alex probably wouldn't let herself join in with us, because of what had happened with Irina a few years back. That had been ugly—but it wouldn't happen again. We wouldn't let it.

Maybe Alex would let the 'ice queen' armor thaw a bit for Kam, though, since there was no possibility of pups. I was pretty sure that with enough lube and prep work, Kam could take her up the ass. Alpha clits weren't nearly as girthy as alpha dicks, though the knots more than made up for it, supposedly.

Through all of these rosy visions of our future pack, I held Kam and let the rumbling thrum of contentment in my chest soothe him. Eventually, his quiet weeping subsided into the occasional hitch, until he finally went limp, giving himself over to me. I liked that. I liked it *a lot*. I also liked the way Leona's hand had crept up my arm to fist the material of my shirt, anchoring her body against us.

"Better now?" I asked.

A slight hesitation, and Kam nodded, not speaking.

"All right," I said. "I need to get Leona some water before she falls asleep. I'll be right back."

I climbed out of the makeshift nest a bit stiffly, tugging my shirttails down to cover my dick since there was no question of getting my fly closed until the knot went down. If I'd been inside her, Leona's muscles would still be holding us tied together—there would be a subtle shift in her pheromones whenever she stopped clamping around the toy, and that would convince my knot to deflate.

The water bottles were lined up on the side table where I'd left them. I grabbed two and brought them back. "Here," I told Kam, pressing one into his hand. "Stay hydrated."

He took it, not quite able to meet my eyes with his red-rimmed ones. "After weeping out a bucketful of water, you mean?"

"Well, that and being held hostage in a cave for six days," I said.

He untangled from Leona enough to roll onto an elbow and drink, while I helped her do the same. She definitely seemed more coherent than she had earlier—probably thanks to getting some decent sexual relief for the first time since her heat had started. I supported her head and she drank greedily, finishing three-quarters of the bottle in one go.

"How on earth did you find us?" Kam asked, sounding steadier now, if still a bit sheepish.

"Combination of military satellite intel and doing recon on a shit-ton of cave complexes in the general vicinity of Târgovişte," I said. "Those crazy terrorist bastards weren't nearly as stealthy as they probably thought they were."

I wasn't about to go into detail regarding how we got access to the intel so quickly... or how badly we'd been freaking out as the days slid by with no success. Thank fuck they'd both at least been alive when we found them. We'd been too late in the sense of Leona's heat and Jax's health, but maybe it wouldn't end up being the irrevocable kind of 'too late.'

"Jax said you'd come for us," Leona said quietly. "He never doubted it for a minute."

An emotion that wasn't the simple kind threatened to get tangled up in my chest, so I changed the subject. "You should be enjoying your knot right now, sweet thing," I told her. "But if you wanna talk instead, maybe you can tell us how this setup is working for you. There'll be at least another couple of peaks coming before it eases off."

She blinked huge hazel eyes up at me, and I tried not to melt like a damned snow cone in July.

"This was... better," she said. "Thank you."

Kam watched her with a worried expression. "Was what I did all right? You're sure?"

She blinked at him. "Of course it was, *odama*. Was it… all right for you?"

"I just want to help," he said, a bit desperately. "To… not make it worse."

"You *are* helping," she replied. "Of course you are." Her gaze moved to me. "And… I'm really sorry, Flynn. It's not that I'm scared of you. It's just that I *cannot* end up pregnant. I absolutely refuse to bring children into this world. Not the way it is now."

"Pups," I corrected, trying not to think of Irina… of the way it had taken both Jax and me to hold Alex down and keep her from running off half-cocked when we got news of the arrest. "Pups, not children."

"Leo's parents are betas," Kam said. "So actually, it could go either way."

That made sense. Beta parents were much more likely to be able to sneak alphomic offspring through the system. Though it was hard to imagine how betas could possibly have whelped such a perfect omega female.

"No, I get it," I told her. "It's fine."

Of course, by 'fine,' I meant 'frustrating as hell.' But I could understand where she was coming from, at least.

With a heavy sigh, Kam set aside his empty water bottle and settled in next to Leona, rearranging her in his arms. "You know, once upon a time there would have been easy access to contraceptives for heats. Omegas could buy synthetic alpha pheromones to manage the peaks, or as sexual enhancements outside of the normal estrus cycle."

I grunted and returned to my place on his other side. "Kinda makes me feel surplus to requirements."

Leona gave a sleepy chuckle.

Kam let out a sharp little puff of air. "That's not what I meant. Just that back then, we could have control of our own bodies, and manage our reproductive lives in whatever way we saw fit. "

I thought of the breeding pens. The plantations. "Yeah. I hear you." Breathing in, I sensed the slight shift in the perfume surrounding us. The ache in my cock eased as my body responded to her cues. "Hey, it looks like she's drifting off now," I said. "You want to get the toy out of her? I'll hang out here until you're both asleep, and then clean everything up for the next round."

Kam freed a hand from his embrace of Leona in favor of wrapping it around my forearm as he met my eyes. "Thank you, Flynn. Truly."

And… damn, but these two were going to be the death of me, coming out of nowhere like a fucking wrecking ball.

———◆———

I kept silent watch over the nest as the omegas slept. Hours passed, and Leona's scent was just beginning to thicken again when the sound of a familiar engine rumbled along the private drive. Grabbing my handgun from where I'd stashed it just beyond the pile of cushions and blankets, I rose and went to confirm through the nearest window that it was who I expected it to be.

Alex climbed out of the driver's seat and slammed it behind her, striding toward the front door. She, too, had a hand on her sidearm—just in case. My alpha instincts quieted from their state of high alert. She looked haggard, and I wondered in a distant and detached sort of way if I was going to have to track down and kill some more people after all, to get revenge for Jax.

I stowed my Glock and went to unbolt the front door, letting out a complicated little whistle that anyone else might mistake for a birdcall before I opened it. Her stance relaxed as she took me in, though she did twitch a bit as the scent of heat hit her.

"Is he dead?" I asked, unwilling to beat around the bush.

She entered as I stood back, making way for her. "He was still alive when I left the clinic."

I nodded once, sharply. "Good. Any other news?"

Her face set in hard lines. "The IV bag Beckett snatched from the lab contained a dilute solution of a novel thiophosponate compound."

"Thiophosphonate." I cast my mind back to our military training. "A nerve agent?"

"Apparently. There are structural similarities to VX agent."

There was a 'but' in there somewhere.

"But…?" I prompted.

She shook her head, frustrated. "But the lab tech seemed confident that this variation wouldn't be dangerous to betas except at very high concentrations."

"The weapon," I said. "The one mentioned in that speech they were supposed to read, that would kill alphas and omegas." It made sense. At least, part of it did. "But you said Jax is still alive."

"Yeah." Alex's mouth twitched into a frown. "Seems like it's not quite ready for prime time yet. Small mercies, I guess."

"They think he'll be okay, though?" I asked.

"They've got him on atropine and pralidoxime at the moment. The IV bag was still mostly full when I ripped the cannula out of him, so he didn't get the dose they intended him to get. The big question is whether there's going to be any permanent nerve damage. It's too soon to tell."

"Shit," I said eloquently.

"How are the civvies doing?" Alex asked, changing the subject.

I shifted mental gears. "About as well as can be expected, I guess."

Alex sniffed the air. "She's getting ready to peak again." Tension lurked behind the statement.

"Yeah," I agreed. "Kam's been doing the heavy lifting. I'm just supplying the pheromones."

Alex raised an eyebrow at me. "You're on a first-name basis, then?"

I shrugged. "He insisted. Can't really argue—once someone's seen your dick waving around, 'Madam Ambassador' and 'Mr. Patel' start to sound kind of silly."

She stared me down, and I tried not to shift uncomfortably beneath that dominant gaze.

"Don't get attached to them, Flynn," she said. "You know that can only end badly."

My jaw tightened. "No, I *don't* know that, *alef,*" I retorted. "You haven't spent time with them. They're special. This pack—we could have something with them."

"No," she replied without hesitation. "We really couldn't. They're unregistered omegas hiding in plain sight at the highest levels of beta government. Do you think the ambassador is going to walk into an international summit with a mating bite on her neck?"

"She could wear high-necked clothing," I said mulishly. "We could make it work. I mean, just look at—"

She cut in abruptly. "That's a special situation and you know it. Not to mention, one that's going to go down in spectacular flames one day, probably taking all of us with it."

I growled at her, my heat-induced frustration boiling over. Alex didn't call me on it, since that was the kind of leader she was.

"What she and Patel are doing is important," she said. "We need them as high-level assets in the government more than you need to get your dick wet. Also, there's the small matter that they'd have to be crazy to risk a mating bond with *anyone*... much less us."

I clenched my jaw to keep from saying anything else, since even I could tell I was still sporting a bad case of knot-brain. That didn't stop the thought from whispering through my head.

But what if they did?

FOURTEEN

Leona

THERE WAS a second alpha in the house. The scent of jasmine and sandalwood drifted to me from elsewhere in the cabin. Still, Flynn was alone when he returned to the nest, just as my need began ratcheting up yet again.

"Alex is back," he said. "Jax is still alive, in case you were wondering."

I held onto enough of the sense of the words to feel a swell of relief.

"That's wonderful news," Kam said, sounding equally relieved. "I hope that also means he'll recover completely?"

"Dunno about that part yet." The alpha lowered himself into the nest, still frustratingly separated from me by the barrier of Kam's body. "Let's not worry about that right now. I'd much rather see how many times you can get our girl off before she takes the knot again. You like that idea, sweet thing?"

My heat rose, cutting off all rational thought as I nodded frantic agreement. And so it began again—the seemingly endless cycle of fuck, knot, sleep. It was no longer the nightmarish hallucinatory haze that it had been at first, but even now, the sense of important things happening around me nipped at the edges of my awareness like a stubborn terrier with a cornered rat.

I was growing more and more exhausted, despite the hours spent dozing between peaks. Two cycles... three... four... and then a long period of blankness before I woke in what felt like the middle of the night. My mind was finally clear, though my body felt like I'd gone ten rounds with a professional boxer.

Also, I was *famished*.

"Ugh," I groaned. "Ow. *Fuck*."

My pillow rose and fell beneath my cheek as someone let out a relieved breath. I lifted my aching head, and found Kam curled beneath me on the mountain of cushions.

"Flynn says your heat has broken," he told me, in that carefully neutral voice he used when he was particularly worried about something. "I won't bother asking how you're feeling."

Memories of the last several days began to filter into my mind, backwards.

"Oh my god," I said. "I... don't currently have enough brain cells functioning to even begin to deal with the burning radioactive fallout from this. Kam, I am *so sorry*."

His arm was around my shoulders, holding me against him. At that, his fingers clasped my bicep convulsively. "Please don't apologize," he said, a bit desperately. "I don't think I can handle it right now."

I nodded, and tried to focus on something practical. "Okay. I'm starving right now. Is there food?"

In fact, I was having a hard time not grabbing Kam's shirt and shaking him until he gave me a blow-by-blow report on what the *hell* had happened in the days since an I.E.D. had blown up our motorcade. Were we still in Romania? What had happened with the summit? If we'd been rescued by our own security forces, why hadn't we been arrested immediately afterward? I gave my head a sharp shake to clear it, and instantly regretted it when my brain sloshed around like a pickled egg in a jar.

"Alex is getting you something to eat," Kam said. "You haven't had any food in four days. I expect Flynn already found somewhere to crash, now that the pheromones have subsided."

"Right," I said, wincing a bit when my stomach audibly gurgled its displeasure. Rather than focus on it, I moved on to the next important thing that I could potentially do something about. "How are you? And please don't say 'fine.'"

"Fine," he said, way too quickly.

"Kameron Patel, I swear to god—" I began, only to be cut off when a knock sounded at the door.

It opened a moment later, and the female alpha, Alex, entered. She gave a hesitant sniff, visibly steeling herself before entering with a bowl of something held in one hand, and a bottle of water tucked under her arm. I glanced down at my body reflexively, but an oversized black T-shirt covered me from neck to mid-thigh. It smelled of stale sweat and spicy alpha.

Flynn.

I was wearing Flynn's T-shirt.

Jesus Christ.

I shoved the realization aside. "Hello. Is that for me?"

"It is… assuming you can choke down something that's supposedly pork and lentils, based on the picture on the can," Alex said. "Spoiler alert—it bears no actual resemblance to the picture. Welcome to rural Eastern Europe."

"If she tries to give you anything containing either fish meatballs or preserved cod liver, run for the hills," Kam counseled.

At this point, I would have considered cat food if she'd offered it. Which, it turned out, was fortunate. I accepted the bowl of steaming, gelatinous, pinkish-brown mush and started spooning it into my mouth without paying much attention to the taste—pausing at intervals to wash it down with bottled water.

"You'll be wanting a briefing on recent events, Madam Ambassador," Alex said formally. She was standing at parade rest a short distance away—eyes front, not looking at me directly.

"Already?" Kam appeared distinctly uncomfortable. "Maybe you should rest for a day or two first, Leo."

"Will that make me like what I'm about to hear any better?" I asked.

"Doubtful," Alex said.

"Then go ahead and hit me with it now," I told her. "Meanwhile, we'll all pretend that I'm not sitting in an omega nest wearing nothing but a sex-stained T-shirt belonging to an alpha—one who's supposed to be chemically castrated, but isn't. First, though, are there any updates on Jax's condition? I know he was hurt, even though I can't remember the details."

"No, ma'am," Alex said. "We've had no outside contact since I returned here with the vehicle two days ago."

Two days? God, I'd been even more out of it than I'd realized.

"All right," I replied, my heart sinking. "In that case, tell me the rest of it."

In clipped and professional tones, Alex related the details of the roadside attack and kidnapping, painting their subsequent rescue efforts in broad strokes—collecting satellite and spy plane intel, then spending days in a systematic search of the known cave systems in an ever expanding grid. I nearly dropped my spoon when her recitation jarred loose my hazy memories of the videotaped speech the kidnappers had wanted us to make, with its spine-chilling reference to a targeted alphomic weapon.

She went on to describe the early findings related to the modified chemical nerve agent that had been given to Jax, and had almost been given to me. Kam, still curled up beside me, wrapped his arms around his knees, hugging himself.

After freeing us, they'd brought us here, to this isolated cabin in the Carpathians that Beckett had somehow magically conjured for use as a safehouse—another thing that didn't add up. Then she and Beckett had driven Jax to a hospital in Bucharest, before dropping the sample of the chemical at a government lab. Once Jax's condition was stabilized, he'd been transferred to a private clinic with a specialist in alphomic medicine on staff, and Alex had returned here with the vehicle.

"As far as the press is concerned, you're both being held at an undisclosed location due to credible ongoing threats to your safety," Alex concluded.

It was all terribly neat... and parts of it made no sense whatsoever upon closer examination.

"What about the summit?" I asked, since her report had been focused on the nuts and bolts of our kidnapping and subsequent rescue.

"Cancelled," she said. "Or rather, postponed. As far as I'm aware there's been no firm date or location announced for a future meeting."

I placed the spoon in the empty bowl and set them aside, lifting both hands to rub at my temples in hopes of banishing my throbbing headache.

"Okay. Let me think for a minute. We should be able to spin this in the administration's favor somehow. Paint this so-called Beta Liberation Front as a symptom of the wider problem of anti-alphomic extremism. It could shift public sentiment, at least back home." I let my hands fall abruptly. "That is, assuming you're not waiting for me to get my shit together and get cleaned up so you can arrest the two of us. Which… I mean, you seem to have gone to a lot of trouble to avoid that so far, but…?"

"You're not under arrest," Alex said stiffly.

I exchanged a glance with Kam, whose expression clearly said, *could you please not pick at this until she ends up changing her mind?*

"Why not?" I demanded, ignoring his silent plea.

"I have no orders to arrest you." The words were delivered in a wooden monotone.

"And you take your orders from Beckett." I studied her as best I could in the soothing red-tinged light of the makeshift nest, but there was nothing to see. That granite poker face had probably been honed in the military alpha program, and I wouldn't be seeing past it anytime soon. "Does that mean he's a sympathizer?" I prodded.

There wasn't so much as a flicker in response. "You'd have to ask him, ma'am. It's not my place to speculate about my team leader."

Her striking green eyes finally moved to mine, pinning me. So close after heat, the alpha power in that gaze sent a purely physical jolt through me, strong enough that she almost certainly saw it. "That being said, you've both got a decision to make," she continued. "The cave system where you were being held had at least two exits, and we're pretty sure some of the terrorists got away. That means that somewhere out there, someone else knows your secret."

Ah. That probably explained why Kam still looked like he wanted to curl up and sink straight through the floor.

"You'll have to decide whether or not you're going to disappear. Maybe start over somewhere out of the limelight," Alex said. "You know it's possible with the right connections—and there's no way you two got where you are today without help from the underground."

While every word of that was true, I had no intention of scuttling off to Jamaica to huddle in obscurity with my parents—not now, when the next few months would be more important than ever. Not after everything they'd sacrificed to hide my omega status. But... it wasn't just about me any more. There was someone else to consider.

"Kam and I will need to discuss that privately," I told her. "In the meantime, though, I have vague memories of there being a shower in this place. *Please* tell me I wasn't hallucinating that part."

"I'll show you where it is," Kam muttered, uncurling from his miserable hunch.

"Of course," Alex agreed. "I'll be outside if you need me, patrolling the perimeter of the property."

With that, she turned and left. Her stride was purposeful but unhurried—and yet, I couldn't help the impression that she was somehow fleeing the scene. When her footsteps had faded and the muffled sound of the front door opening and closing reached us, I turned to regard my packmate.

"I think she's been really uncomfortable scenting you," Kam said. "She wasn't in here at all, if you're wondering. Not in the nest. Not... *during*."

My utter and complete mortification at what I could remember of the past few days threatened to rise up and swallow me whole, but I didn't have time for it.

"Okay," I said. "Good to know, I suppose. Now, about that shower?"

But he stopped me from rising with a hand on my arm. "Leo. *Odama*. Please—I need to know. Are we... okay? You kept telling me it was all right... what I was doing. But you weren't yourself, and I still don't know if—"

"Kam." My voice was as soft as I could make it. My heart ached for him, once I pulled my head out of my ass long enough to consider what he must have been going through these past horrible days. I scooted forward and wrapped my arms around him. "Of course it was all right. You kept me from unraveling... from boiling away until there was nothing left. My dearest heart... of *course* we're okay."

The tension in his shoulders flowed out, on the back of a heavy sigh of relief. His arms wrapped around me in turn, squeezing so tight that I couldn't breathe for a moment. He tucked his face against the crook of my neck, and I felt his lips press a kiss over the sensitive skin covering my mating gland. It was still inflamed after my estrus cycle, and the nerves throbbed with wanting under the light touch.

I thought of what he'd said earlier—that I hadn't been myself during heat. "You're wrong, though," I whispered against the shell of his ear. "I *was* myself. In fact, it's probably the first time in fifteen years that I've been who I was born to be."

"Me, too," he said unsteadily. "Oh, Leo. What are we going to do?"

I stroked his beautiful black hair. "We'll talk about the rest of it later. But right now, *odama*, we're going to take a shower."

FIFTEEN

Leona

IT WASN'T THE Hotel Epoque in Bucharest by any stretch of the imagination, but there was soap, shampoo, and a towel. I wasn't sure if Kam would want to shower with me or not, and in the end, he didn't. It was pretty likely that he'd been glued to my side continuously for the last week or more. I couldn't blame him for needing a bit of space.

Wonder of wonders, Alex had brought our—admittedly slightly battered—luggage along with her when she'd returned from Bucharest. They'd been able to salvage it from the destroyed car, apparently, and the Samsonite suitcases and carry-ons had, in fact, lived up to the promise of toughness from the over-the-top TV commercials. I scrabbled at the zippered interior pocket of my carry-on with shaking fingers and drew out an innocuous looking bottle of painkillers.

The irony wasn't lost on me as I shook them out on the top of the dresser and started sniffing them one by one. The heat-blocker mocked me when I found it about halfway through the bottle's contents... but it would still be useful three months from now, for my next heat. I put it with the normal pills and kept going until I found one of the pheromone suppressors, which I swallowed dry.

It bothered me inordinately that I would have to get used to taking my suppressors on a different day of the week than I'd been doing for the past fifteen years.

Nevertheless, in an hour or two, all trace of my omega perfume would be gone. Back to normal. The thought shouldn't have made me cringe the way it did.

Freshly showered and dressed in something that didn't smell like an alpha in rut, I made my way to the cabin's front room, figuring I could wait there for Kam to get out of the shower. Unfortunately, I hadn't banked on finding Flynn sprawled across the battered sofa, fast asleep.

My scent wasn't suppressed yet, so it was with a sense of inevitability that I watched him blink awake from his post-heat snooze.

"Hey. Good morning, sweet thing," he said, the gravel of sleep roughening his deep voice.

Something low in my belly clenched, and I silently cursed all things hormonal and heat-related. It suddenly seemed deeply unfair that I knew exactly how his cock looked right after he'd come all over himself and popped a knot.

"Good morning," I said, frankly amazed when the words didn't emerge breathless and girly-sounding.

He rolled into a sitting position, muscles rippling beneath dark brown skin. He was wearing a T-shirt identical to the one I'd woken up in, along with black, military-style pants.

His feet were bare.

"Oh, shit," he said. "Sorry. Alex says I'm supposed to start calling you Madam Ambassador again. Blame it on the heat hangover, I guess."

I swallowed, reaching for professionalism and probably falling several miles short. "While I'd appreciate that in public, it does seem a bit ridiculous in private. Maybe we can compromise on Leona."

A smile tugged at his sensuous lips. "Sure thing, Leona. I'd like that." He scrubbed a hand over his close-shorn black hair and stretched, vertebrae popping.

I tried not to stare.

"How are you feeling?" he asked. "Are you hungry?"

My body feels like it's been turned inside out seemed like a bit too much information, so I ignored the first question in favor of the second. "I think my stomach's still processing the canned pork mush Alex brought me earlier, honestly." With a deep breath, I plunged onward. "I wanted to thank you. Not just for agreeing to help me without taking advantage... but also for watching over Kam. I can't imagine what he's been through emotionally since this mess started."

Flynn nodded, not trying to sidestep the subject or make it out to be no big deal. "He's strong, Leona. He'd have to be, to survive what they did to him as a pup. I just let him be an omega for a bit, that's all."

"I know," I told him. "But it still means a lot to me."

Flynn leaned back, resting his arms along the sofa back as he regarded me. He was taking up space—all alpha—and my omega was here for it no matter how hard I tried to push her back inside her box.

"What will you do now?" he asked.

The weight of the world came crashing back, slamming the lid of the box shut.

"I'll need to discuss that with Kam, once we've both had a little more time to recover," I said carefully. "But at a guess, we'll keep doing pretty much what we've been doing—hiding in plain sight, trying to make a difference. Kostya Nikolayev and all the other monsters like him are still out there. So is the Beta Liberation Front, apparently—and at this point, that might almost be worse."

"Back to saving the world, then," he said.

I narrowed my eyes at him, but I couldn't detect any sarcasm in his tone. Still, something about his words rankled. "You disapprove?"

His eyebrows shot up, as though I'd surprised him.

"No—I don't disapprove. I just don't want to see the pair of you get killed. You really think you can go it alone forever? Sooner or later, something bad's going to happen."

"Something bad already happened," I pointed out. "*Lots* of bad things happen, everywhere, all the time. That's the point. But Kam and I managed for years. We'll keep on managing."

Until we can't anymore. The words were unspoken, but they hung in the air.

He leaned forward intently, elbows resting on knees. "All I'm saying is, you two don't have to be alone. You could have a pack."

Warning klaxons sounded in my head. "We already have a pack," I said flatly.

He didn't break eye contact. "You could have *our* pack. Both of you."

Flashing red lights joined the klaxons. *Danger, Will Robinson!*

"That sounds like a good way for all five of us to get killed." I paused. Took a breath. "Besides, I don't get the impression everyone in your pack would be on board with that proposal."

"Alex will get there eventually," he said, with the same utter certainty Jax had said, '*My pack will come for us.*' "It's hard for her because of stuff that's happened in the past. That's all."

I absolutely refused to acknowledge the bitter pang of yearning I felt at the idea of Kam and I being courted… being pursued by a pack of strong, reliable alphas who would pledge to protect and cherish us. Kam loved to talk about the old ways when we were cuddled together, alone in our temporary, makeshift nests—but that part of our culture no longer existed. It had been replaced by breeding pens, involuntary sterilization, and a furtive life spent hiding in the shadows.

"I don't think something like that would be practical, given the circumstances," I said carefully.

He smiled at me, sweet and open. "That's a whole lot of words that don't include 'no,' so I'll take it for now."

I opened my mouth to force out something a little less wishy-washy, but the front door opened abruptly before I could. Alex swept in with a face like a storm cloud.

"*Flynn*," she snapped. "We talked about this."

The whipcrack of her voice had my eyes darting to the side, my head tilting to bare my throat to her submissively without pausing to check in with my brain first. I felt the other two notice my lapse, even as mortification flooded me. Quickly, I jerked my posture straight and my eyes front and center, but it was too late. They'd already seen the supposedly cool-headed ambassador rolling over and exposing her belly at the first hint of an alpha's bark.

Alex's cheeks flooded red with a level of mortification equal to my own, and she straightened to military attention, eyes forward and staring into the middle distance. "My apologies, Madam Ambassador. Flynn wasn't supposed to bother you with that kind of nonsense."

Alpha hearing must have picked up the topic of conversation even through the walls of the cabin. If nothing else, it confirmed what I'd already guessed — Alex had no part in Flynn's crazy offer.

"You know I'm right about this, Alex," Flynn said. "But that's okay. I can be patient."

"I think there have been a lot of phero-mones flying around for the past few days," I began, channeling the same omega ego-soothing instincts that had made me a top dip-lomat. "And before that, a lot of crisis-induced adrenaline. Any omega would be lucky to have a pack like yours... but that's not the world we live in anymore. Kam and I are try-ing to ensure that world can exist again someday — and unfortunately, that means avoiding any entanglements that might be used against us by those who want to destroy our people. I *am* sorry, Flynn."

He gave me a fond look. "I still didn't hear a 'no' in there — so it's all good, Leona."

Alex shot him a quelling glare before re-turning her attention to me. "What you're doing is important. Don't let anyone distract you from it. And... let me apologize for bark-ing earlier. You're right that things have been... *intense*, lately."

I tried on a smile for her. "I think you're allowed a free pass for minor infractions after you've helped save our lives."

"I'm just glad we got there in time," she said. "You should rest for a bit more, and once you're ready, we'll head back to Bucharest. I assume you have pheromone suppressors hidden in your luggage?"

"I do," I confirmed. "I should be good to go on that front in another couple of hours. Kam and I need to have a serious talk, and I should probably try to eat something else first—assuming there's something free of both cod liver and fish meatballs. We can leave anytime after that."

"Very good, ma'am," Alex said. "I'll make sure everything's ready to go whenever you are."

I nodded acceptance, and tried not to feel Flynn's eyes on me as I turned and left the room.

<hr>

I found Kam in the bedroom. The nest had been disassembled—the mattress and bedding back in place on the bed frame; the furniture rearranged. The couch cushions must have been returned to the front room earlier so that Flynn would have something to sleep on other than the bare floor. The lamp, now uncovered, cast harsh yellow light around the room rather than mellow, reassuring red.

Something deep inside me raged at the loss of our ridiculous jury-rigged nest. I shoved that instinct back into its box as well.

Respectable beta ambassadors weren't allowed to have nests. Respectable beta ambassadors didn't *need* nests.

Kam sat on the edge of the bed, dressed in slacks and shirtsleeves as he stared at his hands tangled together in his lap. I entered the room and settled next to him, letting my shoulder brush his. He looked up at me from beneath dark lashes—always so beautiful, even with the old sadness shining from his depthless brown eyes.

"Did Flynn talk to you?" he asked.

"Yes," I said simply.

"He asked you if we'd join his pack?"

I nodded. "So… he talked to you, too." For some reason, the idea raised a sense of disquiet inside me.

"Yes. There wasn't a lot to do in the nest except talk—at least when you were resting between peaks." Kam licked his lips and looked down again. "You told him no, I'm assuming."

I'd told Flynn everything *except* no. My unease deepened. "It's impossible. Too dangerous for us. Too dangerous for them. Beckett might be some kind of closet sympathizer—but what do you think would happen when he found out? And he would, sooner or later."

"What if we all left together, though?" Kam asked, and the bottom fell out of my stomach as I realized he was seriously considering it.

"You want to do it," I said faintly. "Oh my god. You want to throw everything away and run."

He looked up at me again, and his dark gaze was pleading. "Leo, it's not safe. People know our secret now. One wrong word, and this entire house of cards could come tumbling down around us."

"It was always going to come tumbling down," I said. "It was only ever a question of how much good we could do before it did! Kam—I can't run away now. *There's still too much to do*. What about the weapon, for god's sake?"

He gathered my hands in his and looked at me, anguished. "I don't want to watch you fall to that weapon, Leo. What if they decide to let it loose at the next summit? We could get out now—go someplace far away, where no one pays attention. Someplace where the Committee's influence is weak. I don't want both of us to die because you were too stubborn to recognize when the game was over!"

I pulled my hands away from his grip, the words cutting like a knife to the gut. "I'm not giving up," I said, barely recognizing my own voice. "Our people need someone to fight for them in the halls of power. Kam, don't make me choose between you and my work."

An ominous silence fell as we sat staring at each other—separated by a handful of inches, along with a gap that suddenly felt as wide as the ocean.

SIXTEEN

Leona

THE FEAR I felt at the idea of Kam leaving me rivaled the fear I'd felt when my heat hit me while we were trapped in the terrorist cave. I closed my eyes, forcing myself to think instead of reacting. God… the dregs of these damned hormones could get lost *any time now*, and that would be *great*.

I was being selfish. I knew that. Kam was one hundred percent right about the added danger to us, and just because I couldn't let it stop me, I had no right to act like he needed to put himself at risk as well. If Flynn had offered Kam the same thing he'd offered me, it probably sounded like a dream come true to him. A pack of alphas to cherish and protect him? A place of safety, away from the influence of the organization that had killed his family, enslaved him, and mutilated him? He'd have to be crazy not to think about accepting.

Opening my eyes, I reached out and grasped his hands again. "Okay. Okay, you're right. Maybe you should consider this. I *do* want you to be safe, *odama*. I want you to be happy. Just… are you sure Flynn can deliver on what he's offering? I don't get the impression Alex is on board with the idea, and we can't know what Jax would think."

"It's two separate issues, Leo," Kam replied in an exhausted tone. "Getting somewhere safe, and joining our packs together. But you're not going to do either one of those things. I already knew that. I'd just hoped…" He shook his head as though chasing the thought away. "Never mind."

"I'm serious," I said, forcing the words past the growing lump in my throat. "Maybe you should go. Find someplace safe. Go to Jamaica. Stay with my—" I cut myself off abruptly, not sure I wanted to let my parents' location slip when we were within range of alpha hearing. "Well, there are people there who could help you settle in, anyway. No one would bother you there."

Now it was his turn to tug his hands free. He scrubbed at his eye sockets with the heels of his palms and kept them there, speaking without looking at me. "I need more time to think about this."

I nodded, even though he couldn't see me. "Okay. I understand. I think we're going to leave for Bucharest soon. I'm not sure yet what happens after that. We're at Beckett's mercy here, and I still have no real idea what his angle is."

"We need to visit Jax and thank him." Kam hesitated, before continuing, "Assuming he's conscious and can understand us, of course."

Christ. I didn't need to wait for public exposure as an omega. Everything felt like it was falling down around my ears right this very minute.

"Yes," I agreed hoarsely. "We sure do."

Could I do this without Kam? I'd have to, if he accepted the offer of safe haven that Flynn seemed to be extending.

The worst part of it was, I couldn't say with utter certainty that these alphas were trustworthy. There were too many holes in their story. They'd saved us, yes. They'd behaved with nothing but honor toward us when we were at our most vulnerable. But they also weren't telling us the whole truth.

Kam wasn't a fool. He'd have realized all of this, just as I had. The difference between us was that he hadn't lost the capacity for faith. Faith in people; faith in the future. Despite everything he'd experienced, Kam could still look at someone who'd helped him and trust that they were fundamentally a good person. I couldn't. I needed proof first.

And right now, I didn't trust Beckett's motives for not arresting us.

It was a testament to how much danger we were about to face that if Kam decided to place his faith in Flynn and his pack, I wouldn't try to stop him. Either way, Beckett had us on a hook if he ever decided to reel us in.

"Do you want to try and rest some more first, or leave now?" I asked, changing the subject. "The others are ready as soon as we give the word."

"Let's just go." Kam straightened with a final rub of his face and rose. "We can sleep in the Range Rover, assuming no one's going to try to blow us up this time."

I took a steadying breath and rose as well. "If they do, I suppose it won't much matter whether we're asleep or awake when the bomb goes off."

"True," he agreed. "You should eat more before we leave, though. I had a poke around the pantry and found something that looks like normal sardines. It's probably safe."

And so, we were apparently going to employ the 'pretend it's not happening' defense, when it came to the potential unraveling of our years of friendship. In my current state, I was fine with that.

"Sardines," I said. "Awesome. Okay, let's do that, then."

<hr>

Less than an hour later, the four of us were rumbling down a narrow mountain road. My scent had subsided beneath the power of suppression drugs, but Flynn's definitely hadn't, and neither had Alex's. I stewed in the spicy floral mix, wondering with a sharp pang if I would ever smell the subtle scent of Kam's lemon and ginger again.

Sleep was out of the question as the vehicle rattled down the bumpy, pothole-strewn road. And despite my exhaustion, my brain wasn't about to let me rest when we reached the relative smoothness of the highway, either.

"Will we be going straight to the medical clinic?" I asked, hoping for some snippet of information that might help me figure out Beckett's motives.

"Yes," Alex said. "We need to report in, and that's almost certainly where Beckett will be."

I wasn't sure if there was anything to be read into that or not. On the one hand, I'd noted the man's almost paternal relationship with his underlings shortly after they'd first been assigned to us. It was natural that he'd be worried about Jax, but would a normal team leader really stay with his injured man 24/7? There was the sample of the chemical weapon to worry about, for one thing… though once he'd handed it over to a government lab, it would probably have fallen under someone else's jurisdiction.

Beckett's only official mission had been to keep Kam and me safe at the summit. With his other alphas guarding us, he legitimately might not have much else to do except paperwork and reports for his superiors in the security division.

Eventually, we reentered Bucharest. The city looked as stately and peaceful as ever, which felt wrong somehow. My world had shifted seismically. It seemed unfair that the fresh chaos shouldn't be reflected externally in the city around me.

The private clinic didn't look like much from the outside, though it did have a guarded gate at the entrance. The sentry spoke rapidly to Alex in Romanian. I had no idea if she spoke the language or not, but she handed over a pass. The man examined it and waved us through a moment later as the gate arm rose. The parking lot was small, with only a few other vehicles in it. Alex parked the Range Rover next to a gray Audi sedan, and we got out. Entering the building required another flash of the pass. The inside of the clinic was decidedly nicer than the outside, with soothing, neutral paint colors and tasteful decorating.

I got the distinct impression that the UFNA government would be paying handsomely for Jax's stay here. Alex stopped at the reception window and requested Beckett. Again, she showed the pass, and the woman behind the glass nodded in acknowledgement.

A minute or so later, the door to the waiting room opened, and Beckett stepped through. He ran his pale gaze over us and nodded in satisfaction.

"Oh, good," he said. "Come on back. He's awake."

We followed, though Kam and I hung back at the door to the private suite while Flynn and Alex hurried to their packmate's bedside. Even from across the room, I could see that Jax looked terrible. His complexion was pasty gray, and he had dark circles under his bloodshot blue eyes. His arms rested across his chest, one of them heavily bandaged. His hands twitched and jerked continuously.

Nerve agent, I thought. Uncontrollable muscle contractions would be one of the side effects.

Flynn leaned on the side rail of the hospital bed and stared down. "Wow. You look like hell, asshole."

One corner of Jax's lips twitched. "Good to know I look better than I feel, then. Next time, don't be so late." His deep velvet voice emerged as an exhausted rasp.

Flynn grunted in irritation. "Next time, get kidnapped and held captive somewhere that's easier to find. You *know* I fuckin' hate caves."

"Not a big fan myself, after this," Jax agreed. One of his legs jerked beneath the hospital blanket, and he gritted his teeth.

Alex reached down and clasped his bicep. "We're glad to see you awake, *alef*. Everyone is safe. You did well."

Jax snorted, and immediately winced. "You mean I nearly got everyone killed. What a goddamned shitshow."

Beckett, who'd been standing off to one side with his arms crossed, spoke up. "You did everything you could. The fault lies with the lack of intelligence regarding the attack on the motorcade. It's a mess, true—but as long as everyone's alive, messes can be cleaned up afterward."

"We'd both be dead if it weren't for the four of you," Kam said quietly.

"Dead… or worse," I agreed, not even trying to ignore the omega-shaped elephant in the room.

Jax's eyes tracked to us, and I wondered if he'd even registered our presence before now. "Madam Ambassador. I'm just glad they didn't manage to pump this stuff into you. Thank the others, not me."

"Call me Leona, please," I said. "And you're stuck with our thanks as well—sorry."

"Is it safe to talk in here?" Flynn asked.

"That's part of what we're paying for in this place," Beckett said. He met my eyes, and I noticed that the livid cut on his face from the car crash seemed to be healing well. "Come inside properly and close the door, please."

Distantly, I wondered if this was it—the moment when he'd make some demand in exchange for his unexpected leniency with us. I followed Kam the rest of the way inside and shut the door behind us.

Don't let other people control the conversation. It was Diplomacy 101. Listening was important—but framing the flow of the conversation in the way most beneficial to you was vital.

"Mr. Beckett," I began, "you and your team have gone above and beyond the call of duty. You've been nothing but professional in your dealings with us. And yet, we both know you're off-script. You now possess information about the two of us that would be catastrophic to our lives should it reach the wrong ears."

"She still thinks you're going to turn around and arrest them," Flynn muttered.

I forged ahead. "It seems prudent to point out that we also have information about the status of your team that could be damaging to you. Your alphas shouldn't have been in a position to help me with my... *situation*. And yet, they were."

Flynn's eyebrows shot up, and I could have sworn his scent sharpened with interest. I willed my cheeks not to heat.

"Oooh," he said, with evident relish. "Blackmail. *Ice cold*, Leona. I knew there was a reason I liked you."

Of all possible reactions, I hadn't quite expected that one. Beside me, Kam seemed to be biting his tongue to keep from jumping in with some attempt to defuse the tense situation—omega peacekeeping instincts still on edge after the past few days. Alex appeared utterly impassive. Jax looked like he had a splitting headache—which, to be fair, he probably did.

Beckett showed no signs of either offense or anger. "I don't think threats of mutual blackmail will be necessary under the circumstances, Madam Ambassador. There's absolutely nothing to be gained on my end from ruining the careers of a pair of highly effective government officials. And given your admirable record of working to further the wellbeing of oppressed groups, I'm confident you wouldn't risk bringing harm to my team simply because they haven't been forced to adhere to a barbaric and dehumanizing law."

I felt Kam flinch next to me. He'd been a victim of that same barbaric law—irreparably so.

This still seemed too easy, and things hadn't magically started adding up. But I'd poked and I'd prodded—first at Alex, and now at Beckett—without finding a chink in their assertion that we weren't going to be arrested and turned over to the authorities. There came a point where pushing the issue any further was only asking for trouble.

"In that case, it sounds like we don't have a problem," I told him, even though I was painfully aware that we still *did* have a problem—even though it was an unrelated one.

"I'm pleased to hear it," Beckett said, with the faintest hint of wry amusement hiding in his tone.

"Since that's out of the way, can we have a few minutes alone, boss?" Flynn asked. "Pack business."

I tensed, trying not to show it outwardly.

Alex closed her eyes. "*Flynn,*" she said, sounding tired beyond words.

"Fine," Beckett said. "But don't exhaust the invalid, and for god's sake, please don't make my life any more complicated than it already is right now."

I gave him another wary look. It almost sounded like he knew what this private conversation was likely to entail. He patted Alex on the shoulder as he turned to leave. Kam and I moved out of his way, and he gave us a silent nod of acknowledgement as he passed by us on his way to the door. It opened and shut, and we were alone with the alphas—a pack who might well be about to steal my *odama* away from me.

SEVENTEEN

Leona

"SO, I HAD this brilliant idea, Jax," Flynn said.

"It's not actually a brilliant idea." Alex still sounded almost as tired as Jax looked.

"No, it totally is," Flynn continued, oblivious. "We have a pack. They have a pack. We should join packs. It'll be great. We can court them, proper-like. Just like in the old days."

Jax blinked up at him.

"Except, of course, for the part where they're in hiding," Alex said with forced patience, "and haven't expressed any interest whatsoever in doing something so completely and utterly crazy."

"They haven't said no," Flynn argued.

Jax followed the exchange like someone watching a tennis match. "They're also standing right here, and might not appreciate being spoken about in the third person."

I steeled myself. "I'm sorry, but my answer is, in fact, no," I managed, surprised at how difficult it was to force the words out. "Not because of any of you, but because I have to keep fighting for change. I want to live in the kind of world where I could say yes to a proposal like that. But I don't live in that world." The next part was even harder to get out. "However, I can only speak for myself. I don't speak for Kam."

Squaring my shoulders, I tried to brace for having my heart ripped out.

Kam took a deep breath. "I'm afraid I must decline as well, though I wish that weren't the case. Leona is my pack. Where she goes, I go."

I couldn't help the little gulp of relief that broke the silence as I tried to get air in my lungs.

"There's your answer, Flynn," Alex said evenly. "Now leave it be."

Flynn's dark eyes pinned me. "For now I will. But Leona... Kam... I'm going to ask you again in a month or two, and eventually your answer is going to be different. Like I said, I can be patient."

"I'm sorry that you have to decline," Jax said. "I'd have liked the opportunity to get to know you both better, even if I understand why you can't do it."

I risked a quick glance at Kam. He looked distant and detached in a way I really didn't like. Despite his decision to stay, I still couldn't rid myself of the sense of everything falling apart around me.

"What about the three of you, though?" I blurted. "I won't lie—with this weapon on the horizon, the smart thing would be to get out of the line of fire, if you've got the means to do so. I have some contacts—"

"We're not going anywhere, Madam Ambassador," Alex said. "You've got your work. We've got ours."

I gave her a reluctant nod, not truly surprised. "Right. I understand."

"Jax, we should let you rest," Kam said. He still didn't sound like someone who'd given up his fondest dream in favor of risking his life for a very questionable return. He sounded... absent. Like he wasn't really here in the room with me.

"Yes," Alex agreed. "Madam Ambassador, if I might have a private word with you first? Pack leader to pack leader."

Taken by surprise, I hesitated for a moment. "Of course," I said.

She nodded, and her green gaze took in the others with a sweeping glance. "We'll be back in a few minutes."

I followed her outside, and she led me down the hall to an empty patient room not dissimilar to Jax's. She ushered me in and closed the door. I turned to face her, unsure of what to expect.

"You're doing the right thing," she said. "I just wanted to tell you that, because you look like you're not a hundred percent sure."

My breath caught, and I had to swallow twice before I was confident my voice would be steady. "No... I know that. Kam and I— we've worked hard to get positions where we might be able to make a real difference. And with Prime Minister Fairbanks in office now—"

"It feels like change is a real possibility," she finished for me.

"Assuming terrorists don't manage to kill all of us first," I added dryly. "But, yes. That's it exactly. Our generation—we have to give up our own happiness and focus on trying to fix the mess. Maybe that way, the next generation can live and love the way we all deserve to."

Something shifted behind Alex's gaze. For the barest moment, she looked as though she'd been sucker-punched.

I hesitated. "I've said something to upset you. I'm sorry—that wasn't my intention at all."

The hard-as-nails security alpha lowered her muscular frame into one of the padded visitor chairs and ran a shaky hand over her face. "Not you, Madam Ambassador. It's just"—her voice cracked on the word, though it was barely detectable—"*Damn it.*"

I pulled up the other chair and sat in front of her. I wasn't sure exactly how it had happened, but somehow in the hours since I'd emerged from my heat haze, I'd come to think of the standoffish female alpha as a sort of ally to my cause of not getting sucked in by Flynn and Jax's magnetism.

"You went through something that the others didn't," I observed, leaning forward in my seat. "That's why you understand that this could never work. Whatever it was, I'm sorry it happened to you."

She drew herself back to the present with the air of someone who'd had a lot of practice at it. "There was... a female omega, when I was in the military alpha program. She was in the administrative corps—passing as a beta inside the damned army, which tells you everything you need to know about her."

I whistled low. *Talk about some giant titanium balls.*

"Her name was Irina," Alex continued. "We fell in love. Jax and Flynn weren't my pack yet, though we were moving in that direction. It probably wouldn't have mattered—they're both idiots when it comes to this kind of stuff. They wouldn't have tried to talk me out of it even if we had already been pack to each other."

Given what I'd experienced personally, with Flynn in particular, she was probably right about that.

"What happened?" I asked quietly.

Alex met my gaze frankly. "We both managed to get leave for the week around her heat cycle. She'd taken black market contraceptives, so we thought we were safe. Hell, we thought we were invincible—out in the world with our fake freedom and our stupid adolescent belief in our own invincibility. She begged for my mating bite and I gave it to her. Fucking knot-brain that I was."

She took a deep breath and let it flow out.

"Anyway, the contraceptives were either phony or a bad batch. She was pupped after the heat. Since she was at least aligned, we figured she could pass it off as a beta pregnancy and get a discharge from the army, even if it was a dishonorable one."

I winced, having a fair idea of where this was going.

"I never learned the details of what happened, but she was exposed and arrested," Alex said dully. "I never saw her again. They must have extradited her to the Committee, because two weeks later, I woke up in the middle of the night to the agony of the mating bond breaking. They killed her, and they killed our unborn pups."

The bottomless ache in my chest that always came in response to hearing stories like this was way too familiar, and I hated that familiarity with a passion.

"They call *us* animals," I said. "But it's them. They're perverted, sadistic brutes, and we have to stop them."

She nodded. "Yes. That's all that matters—stopping them. But you need to understand. I don't want Jax or Flynn waking up in the night to that kind of horror. That feeling—the sense of the bond stretching and twisting until it's torn out by the roots—I want to make sure they *never* find out what it's like."

My eyes burned in response to the desolation in Alex's tone. I blinked, and two tears spilled over. Moving slowly enough that she'd have plenty of time to pull away, I lifted my hand and stretched forward, cupping her jaw.

"I understand," I said, and her fingers came up to tangle with mine.

She closed her eyes, and nodded. We stayed that way for a handful of heartbeats before she let her hand drop and straightened away from the touch.

"It's in the past," she said. "Let's just try to make sure there's not a repeat in the future."

I hadn't been wrong about her being an ally—but I hadn't understood how determined she was to keep our packs separate. It wasn't only about protecting Kam and me. It was about protecting her own pack as well.

"Agreed," I told her wholeheartedly.

———◆———

Three days later, the specialist at the clinic decreed that Jax was stable enough for air transport back to Montreal. Beckett had spent a good part of that time drilling a coherent story into all three of us, in anticipation of the inevitable debriefing we were about to face. As it turned out, that was a very good thing indeed.

Stepping off the charter plane at Montréal-Mirabel International Airport felt deeply surreal. Jax was still being wheeled off the plane on his medical gurney when Kam and I were whisked away by government security officials dressed in dark suits. I crushed the flutter of irrational panic that threatened to grab me by the throat when we lost sight of Beckett and the alphas.

Two of the security operatives retrieved our luggage for us. We both refused the offer of medical attention. Given a choice, I would have scurried home to my converted loft and hidden under a blanket for a week. Unfortunately, our escorts had other ideas. A black limo delivered us directly to the Foreign Service building, where we spent the next four hours putting Beckett's creatively edited story of the kidnapping to the test in separate interview rooms.

Not for the first time, I wondered if Beckett had actually gotten any kind of official sanction for his rescue operation. On the one hand, if he hadn't, I was at a loss as to how he could have gained access to the kind of intelligence that had allowed him to find us. On the other hand, that simply wasn't how the military chain of command worked. Government security wasn't even *part of* that chain of command.

Whatever the case, I dutifully parroted the story I'd been fed, no matter how many different ways the interviewer framed the questions. At the end, I walked out with an appointment for mandatory trauma counseling and two weeks of leave—both of which I was dreading. The limo dropped Kam at his modest apartment in Little Burgundy, and me a bit farther south in my considerably less modest apartment in Saint-Henri, next to the Lachine Canal.

The driver helped me take my luggage up and gave me a polite nod before leaving me alone.

Just like that, it was over.

The silence inside the renovated warehouse loft echoed. There was nothing and no one here to greet me. No roommates, no pets, not so much as a goldfish. I would need to get groceries. I would need to call the cleaning service and let them know I was back.

Instead of doing either of those things, I stood in the entryway with my luggage at my feet and stared into the middle distance for a very long time indeed.

EIGHTEEN

Leona

I'D BROKEN my relationship with Kam. That realization had grown increasingly clear after our return, as the weeks rolled into months. The worst part was, I couldn't quite put my finger on what had changed—only that *something* had.

He was as sweet natured as always. As polite as always. As kind and compassionate as always. And yet, he was no longer *my Kam*. At first, I tried to broach the subject… to find out if there was something I needed to do, or not do, that would make everything all right again. He seemed bewildered by the idea that there was anything wrong in the first place.

It didn't even feel as though he were trying to passive-aggressively punish me for saying no to the alphas. That simply wasn't the way his brain worked. The two of us had just… changed. Something had shifted, and I didn't like it. Not one bit.

Kameron Patel had been through hell while I was still living safely in my parents' house, playing with Barbies and having sleepovers. He'd cut out large pieces of his own psyche in order to function through a childhood and adolescence that had been nothing short of unspeakable. I had the horrible sense that I was watching another piece of him drift away before my eyes, and it terrified me to contemplate how much more he might have left to lose before he would be nothing but an empty shell.

In the depths of night, alone in my ever-so-normal, beta-style bed, I thought maybe I should have said yes to Flynn, if only to make Kam happy. Or maybe Kam had been right and we should have run, with or without the alphas. We could be in Jamaica now, lying on the beach and sipping drinks with little umbrellas in them. We could be hidden safely away with my parents, far from the world that wanted to kill or enslave us.

These were not good thoughts to be having—especially not on the eve of the stripped-down summit that would pit my powers of persuasion against two powerful Committee chairmen, with the future of UFNA alphomic policy on the line. I needed my brain in the game and my *odama* at my back—not the weight of this nagging guilt and uncertainty.

At least we would be on home territory this time. After the shitshow in Romania, these were to be bilateral talks between Prime Minister Fairbanks' progressive administration and the Committee's top two officials—Kostya Nikolayev and the head of the pan-American region, Enoch Sloane. On the table were several relatively minor policy debates, including expanding the roles of alphas in the military. But the centerpiece of the talks would revolve around the current alphomic extradition treaty.

The god-awful agreement—one that allowed accused alphas and omegas to be sent across international borders to face trial and execution by a Committee-led tribunal—was number one on my personal hit list. Challenging that law had been important to me for a long time, but it had soared straight to the top of my priorities after hearing Alex's story.

I had a small arsenal of pre-approved concessions ready to deploy in the pursuit of my—of the *administration's*—goals. Some of them were innocuous. Some of them stuck in my craw. All of them could be valuable in negotiating for the bigger prizes.

If only I weren't still an emotional wreck beneath my brittle veneer of professional competence.

It had been slightly more than two months since the kidnapping. Flynn hadn't made good on his promise to court us further, and I suspected that was down to Alex's influence. I'd quietly kept tabs on Jax's recovery from afar, not trusting myself to visit him in person as he slowly recuperated from exposure to the experimental nerve agent. As of ten days ago, he'd returned to limited duty, though my contact indicated he was still suffering from frequent migraines and intermittent muscle weakness on his left side.

I'd been half-hoping and half-dreading that Beckett's team might be present during the summit—either assigned to us, or to some other UFNA official. But Beckett was out sick at the moment. With Jax on light duty and their beta chief unavailable, there'd been no question of assigning the team to such a high-level function.

The meetings were to take place at the historic St. Paul Hotel in the heart of Old Montreal, not that I expected the grand surroundings to make much of an impression on the dour Committee leaders.

I'd watched Enoch Sloane and Kostya Nikolayev become notorious rivals over the course of the past few years, rising to power in the organization at roughly the same time but on different continents. They were both seriously terrifying bastards, but I was ready and willing to play them against each other if it would help me get what I wanted.

I would do this, no matter that the rest of my life had become a slow-rolling dumpster fire. Despite whatever wrong turn our personal relationship had taken, Kam and I would grasp the opportunity we'd been given, and we would turn it into real change for our people.

The morning of the summit dawned chilly and gray. I'd been up since four, and Kam had joined me for final prep work over strong coffee at five-thirty.

"I still don't like these concessions related to genetic testing," he said, frowning at the notes I'd jotted the day before.

"I don't like any of it," I told him, shuffling papers. "But it's like any battle. It's best we have a fall-back position ready in case the enemy gets the upper hand."

"I know," he said, resigned. "I know."

We arrived at the hotel an hour before the official start time and began circulating—getting a feel for the undercurrents swirling beneath the surface. Prime Minister Fairbanks and his wife made their entrance a few minutes before the first round of meetings were called to order. Tall, dark, and charismatic, Fairbanks delivered an opening speech carefully calculated to appeal to the news outlets, replete with easily digestible sound bites that reinforced his coalition government's dedication to improving the lot of all UFNA residents, regardless of sex or gender.

"In conclusion," he said, his deep voice rolling around the cavernous event space, "I hope that these meetings may function as an open exchange of ideas, ushering in a new era of cooperation and respect between the UFNA and the Committee."

Respect, I thought, with heavy irony. *Right. Somehow, I doubt that.*

Polite applause ensued. The Prime Minister was bustled out immediately afterward, no doubt heading off to deal with the next item on his busy itinerary. Enoch Sloane rose to take the speaker's lectern. I wondered if he and Nikolayev had flipped a coin to decide who got to play to the cameras by delivering the opening remarks.

Sloane was a plain-faced man with exceptionally pale blond hair. He had the air of an Alabama fundamentalist preacher, with his drawling Southern accent, his forehead shiny with sweat, and the light of fanaticism in his whiskey-brown eyes. All he needed was a Bible to thump.

I exchanged a glance with Kam, who looked vaguely ill as the man droned on about gender impurity and the importance of rooting out the alphomic cancer at its source.

"They would have been smarter to let the Mad Russian go in front of the cameras," he murmured, too low to reach any ears but mine.

He wasn't wrong. Nikolayev might disdain designer suits and the fancy trappings of elegance, but he had the power of charisma in a way that Sloane decidedly did not. I was already making a mental list of the ways Sloane's lackluster public speaking performance could work in our favor.

He rambled on for a bit longer, ending with a story about an immigration official who'd been exposed as an unregistered alpha, and who'd been secretly facilitating the transfer of alphomic refugees to South America. A familiar scare tactic piece, but I had no doubt that it would play gangbusters with the hard-line conspiracy theory crowd.

I took a moment to mourn the loss of yet another link in the fragile chain of the alphomic underground—that shadowy association of alphas, betas, and omegas who made it possible for some of us to escape what would otherwise be our fate. Members of the underground had helped Kam escape slavery and forge a new identity in a new country. They provided my heat blockers and pheromone suppressors. Their ranks included doctors willing to forge misleading medical reports, and midwives willing to whelp pups from non-aligned omegas in secret.

Without them, we couldn't survive. And yet, the underground always felt like such a tenuous web… one that might unravel the moment the wrong thread was pulled.

The summit inched forward with agenda-setting and last minute scheduling changes, before eventually settling into the real work. The first day consisted of low-level negotiations and workshopping. The second day moved into the nuts and bolts of hammering out changes to existing agreements and feeling out where the sticking points lay.

It was a grind. There were a lot of sticking points.

The third day was make or break. Throughout the meetings, I'd felt the imagined weight of Sloane and Nikolayev's gazes on me, making my skin clammy and the fine hairs on my neck prickle. Beneath the fragile facade of civility, they were predators, while Kam and I were prey. If they sniffed us out, we'd be crushed between their jaws in an instant.

They say Nikolayev can smell an omega at twenty paces, even with suppressors.

That ridiculous piece of fearmongering floated through my mind as the man in question approached the table where I was attempting to discuss the finer points of omega sterilization laws with a Committee aide.

"Ambassador McCready," Nikolayev said, sending the aide scurrying away with an abrupt gesture of one hand. "A word in private, if I may."

Kam looked up sharply.

I steeled myself not to react beyond a raised eyebrow, despite the chill that shivered through me at the idea of being alone with a man who'd murdered his own omega sibling in cold blood.

"Chairman Nikolayev." My tone was admirably cool. "Are you sure you wouldn't care to invite Chairman Sloane into this discussion as well?"

It was a dig, and he probably knew it. His lip curled in distaste, but he only said, "Definitely not. I require clarity and brevity. Not saber-rattling."

I ignored the rigid tension in Kam's shoulders, because inadvertently drawing Nikolayev's attention to it wouldn't be good for either of us. This was the path I'd chosen. If it meant a private tête-à-tête with a monster, then so be it.

"Certainly," I replied, as though my skin weren't crawling at the prospect.

They say his sister's body had been almost unrecognizable after he'd finished with her. They say as a young man, he hunted captured omegas for sport, like animals.

I rose, not daring to meet Kam's eyes for what I might see there. Nikolayev ushered me to a private salon adjacent to the event space with old world courtesy that was bitterly incongruous in a murderer.

He closed the doors behind us, and I willed my heart not to start thundering like a cornered rabbit's. When he turned, it was to regard me with a slight frown furrowing his brow.

"You appear to have recovered well from your tribulations outside Târgoviște," he observed.

Ice rolled through my veins. "Yes, thank you," I replied, willing my voice to remain calm. "You mentioned something about brevity and clarity, Chairman?"

Steel-gray eyes bored into me, and the silence stretched for a painful moment.

"The Committee will not bend when it comes to the renegotiation of the alphomic extradition treaty," he said.

"That's not acceptable," I told him without hesitation, a different kind of tension creeping into my spine. "The Fairbanks administration is determined to gain at least some concessions on the matter, especially relating to extenuating circumstances in individual cases."

"That will not happen," he replied. "And if the UFNA attempts to withdraw from the existing extradition agreement unilaterally, the Committee will ensure that your current Parliamentary coalition falls apart, forcing a new election."

I stared at him, my stomach sinking. "That's blatant manipulation of a foreign power's internal governance."

"Yes," he agreed. One shoulder lifted in a barely perceptible shrug.

Right. Apparently the gloves were off now. I could play that game, too.

"I find it interesting that you are the one delivering this ultimatum, and not your pan-American counterpart. I would have thought UFNA treaties were more in his jurisdiction than yours."

Nikolayev regarded me with steely, reptilian eyes. "In matters of policy, my colleague and I speak with one voice."

"Except for the saber-rattling?" I suggested. A strange sense of detachment washed over me, my fear retreating to a distant point, somewhere out of my reach. "He's a liability, you know. *You* understand how to play the game of public opinion. He doesn't. He can only appeal to the fanatics, but you need to keep more than the fanatical base on your side. You need moderates."

Nikolayev raised an eyebrow. "My dear ambassador, I could not agree more with your assessment. However, it has no relevance to the discussion at hand."

I tilted my head. "You're wrong. It does. You can try to dismantle our Parliamentary coalition. But in return, we can bring our influence to bear in an effort to support Sloane over you—putting the weaker leader in a preeminent position, which will ultimately undermine the Committee in the long term."

The corners of Nikolayev's lips twitched upward, though his face remained cold. "You could do so, yes. And then we would see which of us was ultimately more influential on the world stage. I don't believe you would enjoy the results of that particular experiment."

I focused on not letting my body language falter beneath the force of his overbearing presence. Inside, though, a chill suffused me... because I knew he was right. One nation alone could not bring down the Committee. That was its power. It was a hydra, with its many tentacles twisted and embedded throughout the world.

"Alternately," he continued, in the light tone of one who was about to offer an unsolicited act of kindness, "you could accept that you have lost this battle, and surrender gracefully—in exchange for which, I will ensure that all of the remaining lesser battles on relatively minor issues fall in your favor."

I couldn't help my sharp, indrawn breath of surprise. "*What?*"

"A concession," he said, "from the winning side to the losing one. Your Prime Minister's pet military program... the loosening of restrictions related to permanent omega sterilization, in favor of reversible methods using drugs... a reduction in sentencing guidelines for betas convicted of failure to declare throwback offspring. Surely such a tradeoff would be to your government's benefit."

I hesitated, stuck for words. He was proposing a straight trade — the single large issue in exchange for all of the lesser issues combined. Frustration swelled in my chest like hot lava — not least because in the end, accepting or declining his offer wasn't my decision to make.

"I'll need to discuss it with my superiors," I said, trying not to let any of those feelings come through in my tone. "I should have an answer for you within the hour."

He gave an urbane nod of acceptance, after which I turned and stiffly walked out of the private anteroom.

Kam looked a bit wild-eyed as I returned. "Well?" he demanded.

"I need a secure line to the Secretary of Foreign Affairs," I said. "Apparently, Chairman Nikolayev wants to make a deal."

An hour later, as the Undersecretary was in the process of drafting the finalized agreement for the approval of the Cabinet, I wasn't sure if we'd won, or if we'd lost, or how I should be feeling about any of it. For his part, Chairman Sloane looked positively sour about the list of concessions. Nikolayev's face might as well have been carved from stone.

Alphas and omegas would still be sent to the Committee for sham trial and summary execution, without any form of legal recourse. But, on the other hand, there would now be a path forward toward the abolition of the barbaric surgery perpetrated on every omega who aspired to a life outside the breeding pens.

We listened impassively to the details as the new treaty provisions were read aloud, including the proposed changes to the sterilization laws. I was worried about Kam. Of course, I was *always* worried about Kam these days. His eyes held that same blankness they often had lately—but we couldn't talk here.

And afterward, he *wouldn't* talk.

The summit wound down. My superiors rained professional accolades down on my head for my supposed brilliance in negotiating so many concessions from the Committee at once. The Cabinet approved the new treaty a couple of weeks later, and it was duly signed by the Prime Minister with much pomp and circumstance.

The night after the signing ceremony, Kam showed up drunk on my doorstep with two dildos, a bottle of lube, a vial of contraband alpha sex pheromones, and an aura of almost manic desperation crackling around him.

NINETEEN

Leona

"KAM?" I BEGAN cautiously. "Let's sit down and have a talk, okay?"

My *odama* looked like he was unraveling before my eyes. I sat him down at the breakfast bar and plunked a large glass of water in front of him. He drank it, still wild-eyed and disheveled. The sex aids sat accusingly on the counter nearby, taunting me from my peripheral vision.

"I need to know," he said quietly—and I wasn't sure if it made it better or worse that he did not, in fact, appear to be nearly as drunk as I'd first thought him to be. "Leo, I need to know what I gave up. And… I need to know *exactly* how much was taken from me."

I sat on the stool in front of him and gathered his hands in mine. "*Odama*, I love you. And I will try to give you anything you need, just like you've always tried to give me everything I need. But I'm worried about you. I've been worried about you since Romania, but you wouldn't talk to me. I need you to talk to me now."

He nodded, and let his head fall forward—chin against chest, fingers squeezing mine where they tangled together. "I know, Leo. And I'm sorry. This... *all* of this—it's just that it's starting to feel like we're building a seawall out of sand, and the tide is coming in. We're celebrating the fact that people like us can be sterilized with chemicals now, instead of having our wombs ripped out with hooks. We're *celebrating* that, for god's sake! Why are we acting like this was some kind of victory?"

I ducked my head to meet his eyes. "I'm not celebrating it. But we're claiming it as a kind of victory because chemical castration can at least be undone in the future. It's not permanent."

Not like what happened to you. The words remained unspoken.

He shook his head. "Everything's broken, Leo—and I'm not sure how much longer I can keep pretending it isn't."

Something in my chest clenched, as the simple statement spoke directly to my deepest fears.

"Kam," I began, and had to stop when it came out as a rough croak. I swallowed hard—once, twice. Then I tried again. "I hear exactly what you're saying. But... I don't know what else to do? It's like... okay, we failed miserably with the extradition treaty. But somewhere there's a beta couple who hid their pup from the authorities, and now instead of getting thrown in jail, maybe they'll just get hit with a fine instead. That's good, right?"

"I know it is," he said miserably. "But, Leo — why does it have to be *us*? Can't someone else do the work now? Who knows, maybe they'd be better at it than we've been."

A faint tremor had taken up residence in my hands and arms. He could probably feel it. We were speaking truths that I wasn't ready to speak, because if I thought about them too closely, the entire foundation of my life might slide into the sea on those same shifting sands he'd mentioned earlier.

"Can we… please not talk about this right now?" I begged. "Because it's late, and there are two dildos and a bottle of black market pheromone on my kitchen counter — and I'm not really sure I can deal with all of these things at once."

He leaned forward, and I mirrored him until our foreheads were resting together.

"I'm sorry," he said. "Yes, let's not talk about this now. I need you, *odama*. I need to be with you tonight."

I knew, on some level, that his words were half of a lie. I was not, in fact, what Kam really needed. That's why there were alpha pheromones in my kitchen. But it was also half of a truth. I needed him, too. My packmate. My *odama*. We hadn't slept together or played at nesting since my heat. I'd missed him desperately, and it was pure relief to discover that he'd missed me as well.

"I'm here," I assured him. "You've got me — I'm yours, always. But first, you'd probably better tell me exactly how much you've drunk tonight."

He let out a little huff of reluctant amusement. "Three gin and tonics — the last one about two hours ago. I'd say they didn't help much… but in their defense, they at least gave me enough liquid courage to catch a taxi over here and spill my guts."

"Gin and tonics for the win, in that case," I agreed, and tilted my head forward until our lips met in a chaste, gin-flavored kiss. "I've missed you so much, *odama*."

"I know," he said. "I'm sorry."

"Don't be sorry," I told him. "Get your contraband off my countertop, and come help me gather up the pillows."

Anything that suggested a permanent nest was out of the question in my apartment, where I often hosted work colleagues and parties. But even betas could have a throw pillow obsession — and every spare surface on my furniture was covered with the things.

The converted warehouse was all old wood and high, narrow windows, with the bedroom tucked in the back. Protected. Hidden away. It was about the best an omega could hope for while still looking normal to betas. We dumped the pillows on the stupid beta-style bed in great piles, turning it into something that could half-swallow us in softness. I pulled a red chiffon wrap out of the closet and tossed it over the shade of the bedside lamp, plunging the room into a low, warm glow.

Kam bundled me onto the mass of pillows, where I sat cross-legged, facing him.

"Tell me what you need tonight," I said, taking his hands again.

He licked his lips and glanced away, before dragging his dark gaze back to mine.

"When you were in heat... when Jax and Flynn were there with us, I... felt things," he said. "It had to be the pheromones. I got hard, at least a little bit."

"You perfumed," I said, remembering that teasing hit of lemon and ginger.

"Apparently," he agreed. "I didn't think I could... respond that way. At least, I never have before. Flynn—he and I talked a lot, while you were asleep between peaks. He said sometimes sterilized omegas could still respond. Sexually, that is. That there were other ways to have sex, even with—" He freed one hand to make a vague gesture at his lower abdomen. "Anyway, I want to try. And with the pheromones, it will be good for you, too. Not like heat, but... not like what we usually do, either."

I nodded my understanding.

The two of us were intimate. We had been for years. But where betas were in sexual season constantly, for unbonded omegas, sexual receptivity was tied to the estrus cycle. Without the presence of an aroused alpha—or at least that alpha's bottled pheromones—an omega outside of heat didn't experience sexual pleasure. Not as a beta would understand the phrase, anyway.

Kam and I touched each other because it felt good and reinforced our bond. It wasn't a way to chase orgasms, because in the normal course of things, we'd never catch them. Slow massage. Sensual kisses. An embrace, skin to skin. That was how we bonded. That was how we comforted each other when times were hard.

What Kam was proposing now was something different. It was honestly outside of my experience—though after my heat, I supposed it was no longer outside of Kam's.

"I want to soak both of us in alpha pheromones," he said, not breaking eye contact. "I want to lick your clit and fuck you with one of those dildos, while you suck my cock and fuck me with the other one. I want to drown in you and penetrate you and be penetrated by you."

My lips parted, as shock at hearing my sweet omega talk like that combined with a heavy twisting sensation in my belly. In that moment, I felt hopelessly incompetent to do any of those things without making a hash of it.

"You want the dildo in your..." I trailed off, aware that he must mean exactly that.

He swallowed. "It's how some beta males do it. I, uh, did some research. And I also douched before I came here, so it won't be messy."

"Okay." I pressed a brief kiss to his lips. "You already know I'm clueless here. You'll have to show me how to do it without hurting you."

"I will," he said. "It's all right. I just want to try. Conventional beta wisdom is to use lots of lube and lots of patience. And the lube is for you, too, since I don't know if you'll make slick or not. We'll only do what feels good. I just want both of us to feel good, Leo."

I knelt forward and kissed him again, longer and deeper this time. He returned it—and whatever else did or did not work tonight, at least I had my *odama* back. I fell into his arms with profound relief and held him tight.

"I love you, Leo," he murmured against the shell of my ear.

"Love you, Kam," I told him, and nipped the side of his neck.

He helped me out of my clothes, peeling everything off a piece at a time. I did the same to him, struck by how seldom I'd actually seen him completely naked. Mostly, he kept his boxers on when we were together, or wore a pair of low-slung pajama pants. It occurred to me that he was making himself vulnerable in a way he usually didn't. He would be exposing his scars to me, up close and personal.

I'd seen the scars on his chest many times, where they'd cut out his extra nipples. They'd healed well enough to be relatively unobtrusive. Kam was a purebred omega, though he didn't like to talk about his lost family. I was a throwback, born to two beta parents, my body barely distinguishable from a beta female's without a thorough medical and gynecological examination. If, god forbid, I ever ended up pupped, I'd be unlikely to whelp more than twins, and two nipples would be plenty to get the job done.

But the purebred lines that had avoided beta interbreeding tended to whelp multiples—usually three or four, but sometimes up to six. Purebred omegas almost always had extra nipples. Kam had been born with four, but of course the beta butchers couldn't let that so-called *crime against nature* stand.

There was also a scar at the juncture of his right shoulder and neck where they'd gone for his mating gland. Ironically, they hadn't bothered to check if he was right or left-handed first. If they had, they might have realized he was one of the seven percent of omegas whose mating gland was located on the left side rather than the right.

Small mercy, since it was unclear if a mating bite would take in the absence of the hormones that his body could no longer produce. Unsurprisingly, research into such things was basically nonexistent.

It was the scar he usually hid that was by far the worst. Kam's womb and ovotestes had been pulled out through his birthing passage, which had then been sutured shut. He could never again have normal omegan sexual relations. He could never bear pups.

And now, he wanted to find out if the arousal he'd felt in response to the pheromones of the heat nest had been a fluke—or if he might still have some kind of sexual future after all. He'd come to me for that, and I couldn't express how grateful I was for his trust.

With a final kiss to the corner of my jaw, he stretched across the bed and retrieved the vial of pheromones.

"Please let this supplier not be a fraud," he joked weakly, and opened the stopper.

A scent of gunmetal and sage wafted into the air, backed by a faintly unpleasant chemical tang. It wasn't terribly appealing from an aesthetic standpoint, but within moments, my body began to sit up and take notice.

"It's real," I said, sparing a brief thought to wonder about the alpha who'd produced it.

"Apparently so," Kam said, taking a deeper sniff. "Though it does make you wonder what the price tag would be for an alpha who doesn't smell like a gun battle over Thanksgiving dinner."

He didn't compare the smell to the mouthwatering scents of *our* alphas, for which I was eternally grateful.

"Lie back, *odama*," he told me gently.

TWENTY

Leona

I LAY BACK, reclining into the soft embrace of the pillows. Kam dribbled a bit of the clear pheromone solution into his hand before sliding it palm-down along the centerline of my body from neck to pussy. He returned to dab a bit of it above my upper lip, directly below my nostrils. Carefully setting the remainder aside, he massaged it into my skin with slow strokes. I stretched, arching into his touch.

After the long weeks of uncertainty in both my private and professional life, I was touch-starved to begin with. But it quickly became clear that there was a reason alpha pheromones were considered a sex aid. Rather than only feeling Kam's touch on the surface of my skin, I could feel it deeper, traveling along my nerves and pooling in my belly.

"Oh, that's good," I murmured. "Here, give me the rest, I want to do you."

I rolled upright and took the vial he passed me, pressing his shoulder back until he flopped onto the pillows. He clasped his hands behind his head, looking up at me in the warm light with wide, liquid eyes. I was struck for the thousandth time by how incredibly beautiful he was with his olive skin, finely sculpted features, and sensual lips. His thick black hair was tousled, and his lithe body stretched out beneath me in lines of lean muscle.

I knew exactly how hard he had to work for that beta-like physique, too. Pouring the remaining half of the pheromone suspension into my cupped palm, I set the vial aside and trailed my fingertips through the pool of oily liquid, using it to draw light, ticklish lines along Kam's throat, collarbones, and pectorals, then trailing it down the centerline of his taut abdomen.

His slender cock twitched as I rubbed the remainder into the thatch of dark, wiry hair at the base, and smoothed my palms up the V-shape delineating hips that were a bit wider than an alpha or beta male's would have been. The entire room smelled of oiled metal and herbs now. Touching Kam's lovely body made even more heat pool in my stomach, and I felt the first pulse of slick dampening my folds.

"Looks like you won't have to share the lube," I told him, and he chuckled.

"It's working, then?" he asked.

"Definitely working," I said, and dabbed my finger on the tip of his nose, making him wrinkle it at me.

I settled myself onto his hips, straddling him, and he freed his hands from behind his head in favor of clasping my shoulders as I leaned over him. We kissed, languid and unhurried, my nipples tingling with little darts of unaccustomed pleasure as they brushed against his smooth chest.

He ran his palms up and down my back in broad, sweeping strokes, dipping a bit lower each time until eventually his hands settled on my ass, cupping it.

"I love your body," he whispered against my lips. "I love how soft you are. I love the curve of your waist and the little dimples at the small of your back." His thumbs rubbed over the small depressions on either side of my tailbone.

I moaned and slid down to mouth at his neck. "I love the way you carry yourself, like a dancer," I said against his skin. "I love your eyes, and the curl of hair that always falls across your forehead when you're distracted."

"Will you help me put the toy in?" he asked, lifting a hand to sweep my long hair back from my face.

"Tell me how," I said, peeling myself away from him long enough to retrieve the lube and the dildos. One was fairly narrow — smooth and slightly curved at the tip, with a broad base. The other was a knotting dildo, similar to the one Flynn had loaned us in Romania.

Kam rolled onto his stomach and walked me through the admittedly somewhat awkward process of fingering him open. He'd been good to his word — there was no mess beyond what was caused by the lube. It was an odd sensation to be inside him. His inner walls were hot and tight and velvety soft. His muscles clamped around my fingers the way I imagined my own passage must clamp around a knot, but I didn't get the impression it was in any way a transformative sexual experience for him.

I carefully avoided the twist of silvery scar tissue behind his cock, not sure he'd appreciate having it touched and not wanting to break the mood by asking. Eventually, the well-lubricated toy slid inside his body without much drama, and I paused to look down at him.

"Is that all right?" I asked. "How does it feel?"

He wriggled his hips, frowning a bit. "I'm... not sure yet. Strange. Full." He levered himself onto his side among the pillows and stilled, as though listening to his body. "Let me get used to it for a bit. In the meantime, I want to see you come for me."

My body tightened at his words, and I didn't argue as he laid me on my back and started kissing his way down, pausing to lick and suck at first one nipple, and then the other. A moan escaped me as his teeth grazed the tender flesh, and another pulse of slick dribbled out of me. His hand ghosted across my stomach, and he cupped me between my legs.

The difference with the alpha pheromones was night and day. I *wanted*, but not with the mindless, animal need of heat. Kam's fingers delved through my folds, the sensation jolting along nerves that normally slept undisturbed.

"Oh, god," I breathed, as his thumb circled my clit.

He gave my nipple a final kiss and straightened, looking down at me. "Do you want the cock now?"

I nodded, breathless. "Yes, give it to me, please, *odama*."

I was still on my back, and didn't feel the urge to roll over and present on all fours like I had during heat. Kam gave my folds a final caress and retrieved the dildo, rearranging us so my legs were splayed open and he was kneeling between them. He winced a bit and caught his breath as he settled into place—presumably when the toy shifted inside his ass.

Kam rested his right hand palm-down on my lower abdomen, steadying me. "You're so wet for it, Leo. You're *dripping*."

That sounded right, because when the blunt end of the dildo nudged at my entrance, my whole body felt like it was melting. I whimpered and curled my hips toward the fake dick, feeling it slide inside me without re-sistance. Kam worked it in and out of me, murmuring endearments and stroking my clit in time with his gentle thrusts.

"So beautiful," he murmured, as my body undulated, chasing the sensations.

I *loved* this feeling, free of the mindlessness and stress of a disastrous heat cycle. "Why—" I cut off with a gasp as the pleasure spiked momentarily. "Why didn't we do this sooner?"

He chuckled, a low, dark sound. "Because it's illegal, probably."

"So's everything—*ah!*—everything else," I managed, past the upward spiraling sensation that was gradually swallowing my thoughts. "When you're us…"

"True," he agreed. "Maybe it's time to stop caring about any of it."

I certainly didn't care about any of it right now. My heart was racing, my nerves tingling. "Give me the knot," I begged. "Please, Kam, I need it…"

Kam thrust in, and my entrance stretched, struggling to accommodate the flare above the base of the dildo. I groaned loudly, writhing, and it slipped inside to the hilt, filling me perfectly. Pleasure crashed over me, and I came hard, clamping around it, the scent of metal and sage in my nose.

"*Fuck*," I wheezed, once the waves receded, leaving me dizzy.

"Wow," Kam said, sounding a bit taken aback. "That looked… good?"

"Good, yeah," I managed. "That was definitely good."

Every breath sent a little buzz of sensation outward from the toy knotting me. With uncoordinated movements, I manhandled Kam around and onto his back so I could get at his body.

I want to lick your clit and fuck you with one of those dildos, while you suck my cock and fuck me with the other one, he'd said. *I want to drown in you and penetrate you and be penetrated by you.*

My inner thighs were soaked. I fumbled my way to his slender, beautiful cock and stroked my fingertips over it before reaching back to tap the base of the dildo in an irregular rhythm. His entire body twitched beneath me. He hooked an arm beneath my thigh and dragged me around until I was straddling his face.

His elegant fingers framed my hips, pulling me down to meet his mouth. At the first stroke of his tongue, my internal muscles rippled around the dildo. I cried out and fell forward, getting a hand around his dick and licking across the head. His answering moan vibrated along my folds.

This was what he'd wanted, and *god*, did he have good ideas. I didn't honestly have any clue what I was doing, when it came to sucking cock. I figured the term was fairly self-explanatory, though, so I wrapped my lips around his tip and hollowed my cheeks. He squirmed and gasped, his length stiffening in my mouth for a moment or two before subsiding again.

We licked and sucked and writhed against each other. Unbidden, it occurred to me that in this position I was basically presenting. A mental image formed of crouching over Kam's face like this while Jax pounded into me from behind, my mouth stuffed with Kam's cock while Flynn took his ass at the same time. In my mind's eye, Alex watched over us from the shadows with a hungry green gaze.

It was too much. With a high-pitched keen rising in the back of my throat, I came again, gushing slick over Kam's face. He made a sound like a sob and shuddered beneath me, still licking into me. An odd sort of mellow, hazy ecstasy settled across my mind. I wrapped an arm around his thigh so I could reach the base of the toy inside him and grasped it, rocking it gently in and out as I continued to suck him lazily.

I don't know how long we stayed like that, but my muscles finally stopped clamping the dildo in place. The scent of strange alpha and chemicals had begun to dissipate, and Kam was still a ball of shuddering tension beneath me. His intermittent, partial erection had faded along with the pheromones, and eventually he tapped my hip.

"Too much," he gasped. "Stop… stop. It's too much."

I shifted off him immediately, and he flopped back against the pillows, looking exhausted. He draped an arm across his eyes and let out a deep sigh. The lower half of his face was soaked with my slick.

He hadn't climaxed.

With the alpha pheromones a fast-fading memory and my higher brain functions returning, the scene quickly lost its luster. We were both sticky and sweaty, stuffed with dildos that were now merely uncomfortable. And Kam hadn't come.

I reached awkwardly between my legs and tugged the toy free, flinching as the fake knot stretched my entrance on its way out. It, too, was soaked with slick. I dropped it on the floor and turned to Kam with growing concern.

"*Odama*," I began. "Kam? Are you okay?"

It was a ridiculous question. He huffed out a breath of rueful laughter and let his arm drop away from his face. "I'm fine, beloved. It felt... good. You're right, we should have done it sooner."

As I had done a moment ago, he reached back and awkwardly pulled the toy out of his body, grimacing as he tossed it onto the floor next to the other one. I lowered myself to lie next to him, and his arms went around me easily. My back felt cold and exposed, despite his embrace—missing the alpha who should be spooning me from behind. I wondered if he felt the same way. We clung to each other for several minutes, until the sticky unpleasantness became too distracting.

"Shower?" he asked.

"Shower," I agreed.

------◆------

It was after midnight when Kam finally left— kissing me on the cheek, reassuring me yet again that the sex had been fine, and promising not to close himself off from me in the future. We'd scrubbed ourselves clean, scrubbed the dildos clean, and returned the throw pillows to their native habitat of couches and chairs.

After he left, I slipped on a nightgown and went back to bed, knowing I needed sleep if I didn't want to end up looking like a zombie during the news interview I was scheduled to give later today. Coverage of the new treaty and the laws that would soon result were gaining traction in the news cycle. Alphomic policy was becoming a topic of dinner table conversation in a way that it hadn't been in recent years. I could only hope that was the first step to a real shift in public sentiment. If that happened, then perhaps our lack of progress on the extradition treaty would end up being worthwhile after all.

My mind circled restlessly, caught between worry about the wider world and concern for Kam. I'd enjoyed our flirtation with sex in the moment, but that enjoyment had soured immediately upon realizing Kam's experiment with his own sexual nature had failed. Blind rage wasn't really an omegan trait, but I thought if I ever found myself holding a weapon in the presence of the so-called doctors who'd wielded the scalpels and hooks on his body, I'd kill them.

Of course, that was a deeply unproductive line of thought. Kam would doubtless be the first to tell me so. I thought about what he'd said earlier, that he'd responded sexually during my heat in a way he never had before. It occurred to me that tonight's research hadn't taken all the variables into account. I was back on pheromone suppressors now. While I was in heat, I'd been pumping out omega pheromones by the bucket load. What if Kam's body had been piggybacking off of that? Maybe it wasn't just alpha pheromones that he needed.

Unfortunately, it wasn't as though I could stop taking the suppressors again—not now that I was back in Montreal and back at work. At least, not without some very careful planning. A vacation to somewhere remote, maybe? It wouldn't have to be during my heat. In fact, it would be much better if it wasn't. There was always danger involved in taking time off at regular three-month intervals. People watched for things like that. But a random vacation? It might be doable, even though tongues would wag if Kam took off work at the same time to go with me.

But at least that kind of gossip—beta gossip—didn't have the potential to be deadly. I fell asleep to half-formed plans for a brief lovers' getaway, and awoke at three in the morning to the sound of my front door being kicked in.

TWENTY-ONE

Leona

I FLAILED UPRIGHT in my bed, torn from that deep, middle-of-the-night morass of sleep by an abrupt adrenaline dump. The sound of heavy, rhythmic crashing against the door pierced straight to the ancient part of my hind-brain that governed survival instincts.

Intruders in the den.

No alphas here for defense.

I tried to wrest back a shred of rationality. There were other apartments in the building… other people lived here. Burglars or kidnappers would have made some attempt at stealth. In the normal course of criminal investigation or arrest, the police would be required to identify themselves before breaking in.

When you were an unregistered omega, there was only one reason someone kicked down your door in the middle of the night.

My house of cards had just come tumbling down. My time was up. I could only be grateful that Kam had already left—though for all I knew, other officials were breaking down his door this very moment.

Heavy boots clattered up the metal fire escape outside, blocking any possible exit in that direction. The same high, narrow windows that gave me a false sense of security in my erstwhile den also prevented the possibility of an escape that way. I didn't keep any firearms in my home—there was no loaded revolver hidden in a drawer next to my bed. No shotgun propped in the closet.

With the benefit of hindsight, that had been a mistake. Not because it would have saved me. Rather the opposite, in fact. Waving a gun around when the SWAT team entered would have ensured that I died in a hail of bullets, rather than enduring the fate that almost certainly awaited me otherwise.

Pulse galloping, I hugged my knees beneath the covers and buried my face against them as I awaited the inevitable. The bedroom door slammed open with the sound of wood splintering beneath the force of a heavy boot-heel. In a daze, I wondered why they hadn't simply turned the knob to open it. The damn thing wasn't even locked.

Boot steps pounded as several men swarmed in, flashlights waving crazily around the room. Even with my face hidden against my knees, the flashes of light through the darkness were disorienting.

"On the floor! *On the floor!*" shouted an angry male voice.

Betas talked about the fight-or-flight response to trauma. For omegas, it was the flight-or-freeze response, and I'd always tended toward freezing. I didn't move, feeling strangely detached from my body, as though all of this was happening to somebody else, and I was merely hearing the story reported secondhand.

"Get your ass on the floor *now*, bitch!" cried a different voice, replete with barely contained glee at the prospect of violence.

A rough hand grabbed my arm and dragged me bodily off the bed, slamming me face first onto the rug. A boot dug into the back of my neck, pinning me, and all of this was still happening to someone else, someone else. The pain, the choking sensation of not being able to breathe properly—that wasn't me. I was looking down on the scene from a slight remove, at the pathetic form sprawled on the floor with her nightgown riding up to expose one bare ass cheek in the wavering beams of the flashlights. Secondhand embarrassment flooded me on the figure's behalf. How humiliating.

"Cuff the stupid cow," someone said.

Rough hands on skin. Arms pulled behind back. Legs flopping uselessly, trying to gain purchase against the floor. Cold metal trapping wrists.

The overhead lights flipped on. The boot fell away. A hand fisted in red hair, twisting.

"On your feet, bitch."

The sharp, burning pain of hair being yanked out slammed me back into my body, and I gasped, scrambling to get my feet under me.

"Leona McCready, you are under arrest on suspicion of being an unregistered omega. You will be remanded for physical examination and genetic testing prior to extradition to the Committee on Alphomic Suppression for trial and sentencing."

I stood mute, an injured mouse caught beneath the cat's paws. Trapped and as good as dead, once they'd finished playing with me. Men in black military-style fatigues were swarming over my bedroom, yanking open drawers and pawing through the small wastebasket. One of them pulled a tiny glass vial from the trash and sniffed it.

"Smells like alpha pheromones, sir," he reported, wrinkling his nose in distaste.

"Bag it for evidence," said the one who seemed to be in charge.

Had it only been a few hours ago that I was curled naked with Kam, warm and safe in a nest of pillows? It couldn't have been, surely. It felt like another lifetime altogether.

"Grab anything else that looks incriminating. We'll let forensics have the rest. Let's get her in the van. It stinks like a damned slave pen in here."

The hands that had been holding me shoved me forward. I stumbled as they dragged me toward my ruined front door. The other apartments were deathly quiet—my neighbors doubtless huddling inside, thanking their lucky stars that they were upstanding betas with nothing to hide from the authorities.

The officers bundled me into the building's refurbished antique freight elevator. I swayed as it started down toward the ground floor, and my knees nearly buckled when it came to a stop, gravity tugging at me. Ryan, the night security desk attendant, stared at me wide-eyed as I was frog-marched past him in my silky, thigh-length nightgown, hands cuffed and hair askew. I met his gaze as we passed, my eyes pleading silently with him for help.

Ryan's lips parted as though he might say something, but then he pressed them together tightly and looked away. No surprise, really. He'd had no authority to stop the SWAT team when they'd entered the building. It wasn't as though he could stop them from leaving, either.

He would have known that Kam visited me the previous evening. Would the authorities interrogate him? Had they done so already?

The concrete sidewalk was gritty and cool beneath my bare feet. I winced and stumbled as small pebbles dug into my soles. An unmarked white van sat parked at the curb. With horrible clarity, it occurred to me that once I was in that van, it would all be over. That was stupid, though. It was over already. It had been over the moment my front door caved in.

Strong hands wrestled me into the back of the van—not because I was resisting, but because my muscles weren't working right. The van had benches running down both sides of the back, and the area was separated from the driver and passenger seat by a metal wall with a window covered in heavy steel mesh. It reeked of stale urine and vomit.

The man who'd dragged me inside shoved me onto one of the benches. I yelped as my weight landed on my cuffed hands, fingers bending painfully. He wrenched my arms to the side so he could get at the cuffs and clipped a hanging length of rusty chain to them. The chain was attached to a bolt in the frame of the van above my head, and short enough that I had to hunch awkwardly to one side to keep the strain off my shoulders. It occurred to me in a detached sort of way that if the van got in a wreck and I went flying, both of my arms would be wrenched out of their sockets—maybe torn off completely.

My guard settled on the opposite bench, arms crossed and legs spread wide, leering at me. His badge was city police, not federal security—not that it ultimately mattered.

"Where are you taking me?" I asked in a wavering voice. "What precinct?"

"We're taking you straight to hell, bitch," he said. He reached down and cupped his crotch suggestively, his grin widening. "But ask me nice, and maybe I'll take you to heaven first, you little omega slut."

The words slid off, not sticking. There was no point in protesting. I was an unregistered omega. I had no rights. It felt odd to think that I'd been in a meeting room with international dignitaries not so long ago, hammering out policy and treaty details. The fact that these two worlds could coexist on top of each other seemed wrong, somehow.

I didn't respond, and the man's expression twisted into anger. He worked his jaw for a moment and spat, the gob of saliva hitting my bare shin and sliding down.

"Stupid cunt," he said. "Walkin' around like you're something special. You ain't special. You ain't nothin'." He spat again. This time it landed on the floor by my feet.

When I still didn't rise to the bait, he seemed to lose interest. The van rocked and juddered as it sped through the early morning gloom, the chain tugging at my wrists when I swayed. After an eternity, it slowed and turned before backing up and finally coming to a jerky stop. The engine turned off, and I heard doors opening and slamming. A fist rapped on the side, and my guard lumbered to his feet.

"End of the line," he said with a smirk, looming over me as he unhooked the chain and hauled me upright.

The van doors opened. The vehicle had backed up to an institutional-looking rear entrance. Dirty brick walls framed steel double doors that stood open and waiting, like the maw of some great beast. Fluorescent overhead lighting glared from within. I tried to crane around—to get a look at the city and try to identify what part of it we were in—but it was no good. The glare was too bright, the night still too dark, and I was dragged inside before I saw anything of use.

There would be no phone call to a lawyer for me. No chance to tap the brakes on what was about to happen. The SWAT officers handed me over to the precinct's intake officers. I was stripped, cavity-searched, dressed in a scratchy gray smock, and handcuffed again. My blood was drawn from a vein in my arm, and I was finally shuffled off to a freezing cell in an empty part of the station. The door clanged shut, and a few moments later, I was alone with the echo of my own unsteady breathing—once more a prisoner trapped in a cell, but this time without my packmate or an alpha protector for company.

Sometime in the coming hours, representatives from the Committee would come. I would be transferred into their custody and remanded for a sham trial. Not only was my life as good as over, but Enoch Sloane would use my case as fuel for his paranoid conspiracy-mongering. I might well have just brought down Prime Minister Fairbanks' government with my stubborn insistence on staying to fight, rather than running when I'd had the chance.

Did they have Kam in custody, too? Was he even now huddled alone in some other bare cell, somewhere in the city?

Would I ever see him again?

I sank down to sit with my back against the sleeping bench with its thin, plastic-covered mattress. Covering my eyes with my hands, I curled forward against the staggering ache of my own stupidity.

"Oh, Kam," I whispered, a barely audible rasp. "I'm so, *so* sorry."

TWENTY-TWO

Alex

"YOU'RE SURE about this?" I asked, my tone flat. Beside me, Beckett kept his hands on the wheel and his eyes on the road ahead as we pulled up to a stoplight in the murky, early morning gray.

"I am," he said. "We've kept our powder dry long enough. Things are starting to snowball out of control. It's time to make a move."

"You don't usually torture your metaphors this badly, Chief," I observed. "I feel like there's something you're not telling me."

Beckett shot me a sidelong glance, kind but unapologetic. "There are lots of things I don't tell you Alex. Unfortunately, it's part of the job description."

I raised an eyebrow. "You do realize that when things inevitably go tits up, you're not going to be able to protect us, no matter how careful you think you're being. What does *You-Know-Who* think about this current mess?"

Beckett's expression soured at the mention of *the person who shall not be named*. "I'll be sure to ask, next time I talk to them."

I stared at him, unblinking. He ignored the weight of my alpha glare, just like he always did.

"I really hate this, you know," I told him in a monotone.

"I know," he said, not unsympathetically. He turned right, pulling into a modest parking garage. "Here we are. Remember—federal jurisdiction, sensitive political situation, blah, blah, blah. You know the drill."

In my case, 'the drill' was to look stoic and intimidating while mostly keeping my trap shut. I'd had more than a decade of practice to perfect that act, after all.

"Understood. You've got the vehicles organized?" That was my nerves showing through, and I silently cursed myself. Of *course* he had the damned vehicles waiting for us.

"All ready to go," he assured me. "We just need to pick up our passenger."

This day had always been coming—even if I hadn't expected it to happen quite so soon. I squared my shoulders as Beckett pulled the black government-issued sedan into a parking spot and turned the engine off. "Right," I said. "Let's get this done."

We exited the car and marched toward the entrance of the precinct, the picture of official business with our straight spines and dark suits. Once inside, my boss headed directly for the front desk and placed his badge on it.

"Agent Rhys Beckett, federal security," he said in clipped tones. "I need to speak with the duty officer in charge, please."

The female desk sergeant blinked at us, evidently not used to federal agents barging in at six in the morning and demanding things of her. "I'll, uh, tell him you're here, sir. Can I let him know what this is about?"

"Official business," Beckett replied un-helpfully. "We'll wait here while you get him."

Still looking somewhat flummoxed, the sergeant turned and picked up a phone, speaking into it quietly. There was a brief exchange that involved several uncertain glances being thrown in our direction, and in due course, the officer in charge appeared. He was a big man, perhaps in his late fifties, and while he'd let himself go after too much time as a desk jockey, he still dwarfed Beckett in terms of both height and breadth.

Beckett extracted the manila folder that had been tucked under his arm and set it on the desk. "Good morning, Lieutenant...?"

"Dupont," said the man. "And you are?"

"Rhys Beckett, federal security service. There seems to have been some confusion about jurisdiction during a recent arrest. I'm here for a prisoner transfer." He scooted the folder toward Dupont with an air of expecta-tion.

The lieutenant's expression closed off ab-ruptly, leaving no question that he knew exactly which prisoner Beckett was talking about. That, at least, answered the question of whether or not we were in time to get her before the Committee did.

She was still here.

"I wasn't informed of any such transfer." Dupont opened the folder, glancing down at the contents. "This was strictly an MPD operation. We acted on information relayed directly to police detectives from a trusted source."

That *trusted source* was almost certainly a Committee operative. If that was the case, the truly disturbing part was that the information on Leona McCready could only have come from the so-called Beta Liberation Front. The fact that the terrorists and the Committee were apparently in bed together was… not good.

"Indeed," Beckett replied, giving the man a tight smile. "However, you may not be fully aware of the… *delicate political situation* involved in this particular arrest, shall we say. The feds' jurisdiction on this one trumps local jurisdiction. You'll find all of the paperwork in order."

Though it looked convincing, the paperwork in question was not, in fact, in order. It was one hundred percent forged. That little factoid would come back to bite somebody in the ass soon enough. Whether that 'somebody' ended up being us or the lieutenant was an open question at this point.

Dupont frowned over the sheaf of documents. "I'll need to speak to the precinct captain."

"Of course," Beckett said, unperturbed. "We'll wait while you do that."

<hr />

In the end, it took well over an hour for Beckett to politely but firmly bully the station commander into acknowledging federal jurisdiction. I was viscerally aware of the increasing number of hostile looks we garnered from the other officers on duty, as muttered gossip spread through the station. I ignored them. My gender presentation as a female alpha wasn't exactly subtle, so I was used to a certain background level of hostility.

Finally, Beckett turned to me. "Go retrieve our prisoner, please. It looks like we're about ready to leave." He shot an expectant look at Dupont.

The lieutenant gestured toward a burly uniformed officer sitting at a desk nearby. "Owens. Escort this… *agent*… to the cells and transfer the omega to her custody."

As poorly veiled disdain went, I'd heard worse. Owens retrieved a set of keys with a grunt of acknowledgement. I ignored the contemptuous look he raked over me and followed him into the back, passing through a series of security doors. Our footsteps echoed loudly against the cinderblock walls. Cameras tracked our progress with blinking red eyes — more evidence that after today, there would be no coming back for us.

Though honestly, considering Beckett was out front signing his own name to forged federal transfer papers at this very moment, the camera footage of me springing a prisoner from jail without any legal standing to do so was probably superfluous.

Owens eyeballed me with clear distaste. "So, federal security, huh?"

"Yes," I replied tersely, having no interest whatsoever in small talk with this beta meatbrain.

"Wouldn't catch the MPD letting your kind onto the force," he said, not taking the hint.

"Your loss," I told him, as we entered a row of holding cells. "I guess there's no accounting for taste."

"Fuckin' hyena bitch," he muttered, trotting out the old, unimaginative slur for female alphas. I let it slide.

He stopped in front of the last cell on the right. The key clanked in the lock, and he jerked his chin toward the red-haired form huddled in the corner, staring fixedly into the middle distance. "So, is she your little omega girlfriend, or something? Come to get your fuck-toy back?"

That one, I was less inclined to let slide. I loomed over him as he turned to pull the door open, using my slight advantage of height with the full knowledge of how much beta men hated that.

"No," I said sweetly. My lips pulled back, baring teeth in an expression that was only distantly related to a smile. "She's not. Do you know how you can tell?"

"Uh…" He took a half-step back, yielding ground without realizing it.

My voice hardened to steel. "Because *you're still breathing.*"

I brushed past him without giving him another glance, trying with minimal success to soften my stance as I entered and crossed to the figure curled into a miserable ball in the back. The cell was harshly lit by the same fluorescent tube lighting as the rest of the place. Bars formed three walls, open and unprotected. It was devoid of anything soft beyond the one-inch thick plastic pad on the sleeping bench—all sharp edged metal and hard surfaces.

Omega hell, in other words.

"Ms. McCready," I said, aware of how stiff my voice sounded. She was no longer *Madam Ambassador,* and never would be again. Looking down at her dazed face, I was once more amazed by how high she and her sad-eyed *odama* had flown before someone finally clipped their wings.

"*What—?*" she rasped, blinking huge hazel eyes up at me. "*How?*"

"We're leaving. Transfer of custody." I had the worrisome impression that she didn't really believe I was here. Crouching, I grasped her arms and pulled her to her feet as gently as

I could. Bruises in the shape of fingers circled her right bicep, marring the pale, luminous skin. She swayed, my grip the only thing keeping her upright for the first few seconds until she locked her knees.

"You got cuffs?" Owens asked.

I raked a contemptuous gaze over him. "Why? Worried she's going to overpower you?"

He leveled a glare of hatred at me in return. "Prisoners are s'posed to be cuffed."

"Then it's a good thing she's not your prisoner anymore," I said, and led my charge out of the cell on stumbling legs.

Beckett met us at the second to last security door, and ran an assessing eye over the smock-clad form in my grasp. "We're going out the back. I'll bring the car around."

He had the manila folder tucked under his arm once more, but no bag or other sign that Leona McCready's belongings had been returned to her. Of course, it was quite likely they'd dragged her out of her home with only whatever clothing had been on her back—and in the middle of the night, that might not have been much.

Whether she'd realized it yet or not, she'd just lost everything—possessions, money, career… *everything*. To all intents and purposes, Ambassador Leona McCready no longer existed. Idly, I wondered what would rise to take the place of that lost life.

The car backed up to the rear entrance where Beckett had left us waiting. I bundled my omega charge into the back seat, stretching the seatbelt across her body when she seemed disinclined to do it herself. But when I reached to open the passenger-side door, Beckett stopped me with a look.

"*Alex*," he said, gently reproving. "Get in the back seat. She's in shock, and you're on omega duty."

I swallowed the argument that wanted to rise, aware that my reaction was irrational even as a sick sense of dread settled in my stomach.

"You should have brought one of the others along—not me," I managed.

He didn't reply, because his words hadn't been a suggestion—and Beckett did not engage in debates when it came to orders. Swallowing my misgivings, I circled around the car and got in the back. We drove away, leaving the precinct and the cops behind, along with their slurs and hate-filled gazes.

Leona, barefoot and dressed in a shapeless tunic, stared with unfocused eyes at the back of the seat in front of her. Montreal was waking up around us, traffic growing heavier as the morning crawled sluggishly toward business hours. She didn't speak. Didn't look out the window. Didn't blink. Her face was an ugly shade of gray, her lips tinged bluish.

I couldn't get anything useful from her scent. She was back on suppressors, of course.

Instead, I reluctantly lifted a hand and brushed the backs of my fingers against her cheek. Her skin was chilly to the touch, like wax.

"Crank the heater," I said. "She's freezing cold."

Air blasted from the vents, quickly growing warm. Beckett fiddled with the center vents, aiming them through the gap between the front seats. Leona shivered as the hot air hit her skin, curling into herself.

Scent or no scent, the aura of unhappy omega drove a knife through my alpha instincts, bringing back memories I'd worked hard to bury. I was not the right person for this job. Beckett should have brought Jax, or Flynn. I made a not-very-successful attempt to modulate my scent into something reassuring. Scooting close enough for our upper arms to brush, I sat stiffly next to the omega who'd cupped my cheek in her soft hand as she shed tears for the pain of my long-ago loss.

By the time Beckett pulled into a long-term parking lot at Dorval Airport, Leona's waxy chill had given way to shivering and chattering teeth. She still showed no sign of real awareness of her surroundings. I'd covered her with my jacket for extra warmth, and tried to get some water into her from the bottle Beckett handed back to me. I was sure Flynn would have had her wrapped up against his chest by now, soothing her with his body heat and an alpha purr. I... couldn't, and I wasn't sure what kind of monster that made me.

We weren't here to catch a flight. Beckett pulled in next to an unremarkable tan Toyota with Vermont plates, and we transferred to the other car. Within moments, we were back on the road. We crossed first the St. Lawrence River, and then the Canal de Beauharnois, taking Highway 138 southwest into New York, where we once again changed cars. Beckett continued south on NY-30, through the city of Malone and into the wilder areas at the northern edge of the Adirondacks.

We passed Lake Titus and entered the Deer River Primitive Area. Beckett turned onto a private road skirting the edge of Lake Duane. The gravel drive wound through old growth trees and grassy clearings, until eventually a house came into view. It was two stories, built into the side of a hill that overlooked the lake below. The outside gave the impression of someone's extravagant vacation home that had been left to fall into disrepair. The area around it was overgrown, and the cedar siding was weathered.

A white Jeep Cherokee sat parked in the weed-infested circle drive. Beckett pulled up behind it and killed the engine.

"Home sweet home, until we figure out next steps," he said. "Let's get Ms. McCready inside. You'll need to carry her—this gravel would tear up her feet pretty bad."

I firmed my jaw. "Right."

No sooner had I gotten Leona unbuckled and scooped her out of the back seat, holding her bridal-style, than Flynn came rushing out of the front door.

"You got her," he said with obvious relief. Before I quite knew what was happening, he'd lifted her out of my arms and into his own. "How bad off is she? What did they do to her?"

"It's just shock," I said stupidly. "You'll need to treat her for shock."

Flynn nodded and carried her into the house, staring down at her like he could hardly believe she was here. I followed in something of a daze, registering that the inside of the place was a lot nicer than the outside would have suggested. Before Beckett had time to close the front door behind us, a familiar slender, dark-haired omega came hurrying into the entryway, with Jax following behind at a slower pace.

"*Leo!*" Kameron Patel said breathlessly.

Leona let out an ugly, gulping gasp like someone surfacing from drowning, and squirmed in Flynn's hold. He set her on her feet and she stumbled forward, half-falling into her packmate's arms.

"Kam," she said faintly, burying herself in his tight embrace. "*Oh, god.* Is this a dream?"

And, *fuck.* I needed—suddenly and desperately—not to be inside this house.

"I'll check the perimeter," I said hoarsely, before fleeing the scene—leaving behind the two sweet, soft-eyed omegas who'd barely managed to escape the same fate that had claimed Irina.

TWENTY-THREE

Leona

AFTER AN UNKNOWN amount of time spent huddled in the freezing jail cell, I slipped into an odd, dreamlike state that was confusing, but tolerable. Distantly, I was reminded of nature programs I'd watched with my family in childhood, where a gazelle or zebra lay peaceful and blank-eyed on the savanna as the lion ate them alive.

Why don't they scream and fight? I'd asked my father, who'd gone on to explain about adrenaline, endorphin loops, and psychological dissociation. He'd finished by saying that we couldn't really know what went on in an animal's head, but that in the end, nature protected its own by whatever means necessary.

I wondered if the dying gazelles dreamed of an unlikely rescue by a towering gazelle goddess who picked them up and led them to safety with gentle hands, smelling of jasmine and sandalwood and worry.

In my dream, I was in a car, two voices murmuring nonsense in the background. My entire body was numb with cold, but then warm fingers brushed my cheek and hot air blew against my skin, making me shiver as feeling began to return to my limbs. The dream kept changing, the car interior shifting from dark leather to tan vinyl to gray velour. An arm brushed against mine, and I breathed in the illusion of a comforting alpha scent.

Maybe I could just stay like this through all of it—let the trial and the pain and my impending death float unimportantly in the background while I remained in an ever-moving, ever-changing car with a stoic, half-seen alpha at my side, escorting me to the afterlife… if there even was one.

The gray-velour vehicle rattled along a gravel drive, and eventually came to a stop. The voices said things in the background, and I wondered idly if the car was about to change again. Doors opened and closed. Hands released my seat belt and strong arms scooped me out of the seat. I had a vague impression of trees and birds and sky. Then there was an awkward shuffle as new arms reached for me.

Musk and cardamom tickled my nose. I knew that scent, too, and decided that if this dream was to be the last thing I experienced before the lion devoured me, I was okay with that.

"You got her," said a deep voice, the sense of the words beginning to penetrate my awareness for the first time since the hallucination had started. "How bad off is she? What did they do to her?"

"It's just shock," said the other voice, sounding hoarse and strained. "You'll need to treat her for shock."

The world rocked dizzily around me as I was carried through a door, the sky and trees disappearing from sight. I blinked in the low light, gazing up at a handsome, dark-skinned face for a few moments until movement caught my peripheral vision.

"*Leo!*" Kam appeared from an interior hallway, rushing toward me.

I choked, the air suddenly catching in my throat, and began to struggle weakly against the arms holding me. They set me down, and it was all I could do to stay upright long enough to stagger toward that beautiful vision, even if it wasn't real.

Arms caught me.

"Kam," I croaked, burying myself in the tight, illusory embrace. "*Oh, god*. Is this a dream?"

Kam clutched my body to him, his arms shaking around me.

"I'll check the perimeter," muttered a voice from somewhere behind me, and I vaguely registered a door closing.

"Leo," Kam said into my hair. "*Odama*. I don't know exactly what's going on yet, but you're safe. It's not a dream, I promise."

"Feels like a dream," I protested weakly, still clinging to him.

"It kind of does, doesn't it?" he agreed, but the solid, shuddering body pressed against mine didn't waver in its solidity.

A strong hand closed on my shoulder, the smell of fall spices once more wafting over me. Another figure approached behind Kam, ambergris and evergreen joining the mix.

"Alex says you're in shock," said the deep voice from earlier, and my mind tossed up a name to go with it. *Flynn*.

"Warm bath, food, sleep." That was cypress-and-ambergris speaking. Another name bubbled up. *Jax*.

"They're right, *odama*," Kam said. "Come on, let's get you cleaned up and fed. We can talk when you're feeling better."

He disentangled enough to get a shoulder propped beneath mine, my arm draped around his neck for support. Another strong arm wrapped around me from the other side, and I allowed myself to be led away on legs that felt like a newborn colt's. We reached a hallway that was too narrow for three people abreast, and after a brief exchange over my head, Flynn picked me up again, cradling my body against his broad chest.

We ascended a set of stairs to the second story. It was a large house, not at all similar to anywhere I'd ever lived or dreamed of living. That was another tally in the 'not a dream' column I was using to informally keep score. But honestly, at this point, the mental effort began to feel like too much work. It was real, or it wasn't. Either way, it was nice. I gave myself over to it, figuring that in the worst-case scenario, a psychotic break was still preferable to facing my fate at the hands of the Committee while in my right mind.

The landing at the top of the stairs had hallways branching off to the left and right. We turned right and Jax opened the second door leading into a bathroom—large and elegant, dominated by a raised platform leading to a massive sunken tub. Jax crossed to the bath and lowered himself carefully into a crouch to turn on the taps, favoring his left side as he did.

"Shower first, while that monstrosity is filling?" Flynn suggested, putting me down and supporting me until my legs were steady. "You won't run out of hot water. The place has a tankless heater."

After spending hours chilled to the bone in my cell, that sounded like heaven. I nodded wordlessly, not trusting my voice.

Jax straightened. "There's shampoo and conditioner and body wash. I think we covered all of the basics. Kam, will you be all right on your own with her? If so, we'll give you two some privacy."

Flynn grumbled something inaudible. Inside my mind, something flipped—a switch clicking from one position to the other.

"You can both stay," I said. I exchanged a look with Kam. "We want you here."

God, I wanted them here. Besides, it probably *was* a dream, so it's not like it really mattered anymore. If I was going to die out in the real world, didn't I deserve this first? Flynn's brilliant smile in response to my words made it all worthwhile.

"Kam?" Jax asked. "That all right with you?"

A fragile expression that might have been hope lightened Kam's features.

"We want you here," he echoed. "Please."

Jax's worried expression softened. He still looked haggard, and I was sorry that my subconscious hadn't restored him to full health.

"Then consider us your spa staff," he said.

Flynn tugged the hem of my threadbare gray smock. "Want me to burn this?"

"Not until I can watch," I said, and tugged it over my head with the unconcern of someone who knew deep down that this wasn't really happening.

Two sets of eyes landed on me appreciatively. Two scents sharpened. Then Flynn's gaze tracked to my bicep, and he frowned. I looked down and saw the finger-shaped bruises there.

"Do I need to break some necks?" he asked.

My mind shied away from that horrible moment when the police had broken into my bedroom. My arm and the back of my neck began to throb, as though my body had suddenly remembered it was hurt. I swayed in place, and Kam's arm came around me.

"Let's table the plans for bloody revenge until a bit later, all right?" he said.

"Yes, let's," Jax agreed, watching my expression carefully.

"Sorry," Flynn said, looking away. "I didn't mean to upset you, Leona."

"It's okay," I said faintly.

Kam stripped down to his boxers and helped me into the shower. It was spacious and clean, with clear glass-paneled doors. Outside, I could see the two alphas watching us avidly for the first minute or two, until the glass steamed up and obscured them. Was this what it would have been like to have a pack? I blinked at Kam.

"I want this to be real," I told him, the words sounding a bit bereft even to my own ears.

He pulled me into his arms again and held me there for a long moment before easing me back. "Let's get the dregs of this day washed off you, okay?"

I nodded, and let him help me wash my hair and body clean of the stench of the jail cell. When we were done, he turned off the shower and opened the door. One of the alphas had laid a trail of towels on the floor separating the shower from the platform with the sunken tub so it wouldn't be slippery. Flynn took my hand and steadied me from the other side as Kam led me up the low steps and helped me slide into the steaming water.

The alpha gave my knuckles a final rub with his thumb before releasing my hand. Kam lowered himself down next to me in the spacious bath. I sighed with contentment and melted against him, finally free of the bone-deep chill for the first time since I'd been awoken by the sound of men breaking down my door.

Relaxation made my body feel heavy and my mind, slow. I dropped into a half-doze beneath the sensation of Kam's fingers stroking through my wet hair, with two alphas on guard and no need for me to stay alert. Conversation droned around me, but I couldn't spare the energy to focus on it. I registered Kam asking, *"Is Alex okay? She looked upset,"* and Jax replying, *"She's going through some things. Give her time."*

At one point, Flynn's spicy scent disappeared from the room, and I peeled open an eye.

"It's all right," Kam said. "He's just gone to get you some food."

I nodded and returned to my mindless dozing, nuzzling my face against Kam's neck. Eventually, he nudged me back into full awareness.

"Come on. *Up.* The water's getting cold, and I'm turning into a prune."

I grunted my displeasure at the idea of moving.

"There's food," Jax said, sounding mildly amused.

My stomach rumbled in reaction to the thought of a decent meal.

"You need to eat," Kam told me firmly, and herded me out of the bath. Jax met me with a huge, fuzzy towel. I dried off and wrapped it around me, while Kam rubbed himself down and redressed in his dark jeans and white button-down shirt, minus the wet boxers.

"We'll do something about the clothing situation within the next couple of days," Jax said. "But for now, Leona—Flynn says you don't object to oversized T-shirts as tunics. Hopefully he's telling the truth about that."

He indicated a large gray T-shirt laid out on the vanity. I lifted it to my nose and breathed in a smell like the woods outside.

"Thank you," I told him, and pulled it over my head, letting the towel fall away beneath it. The shirt hung to my thighs.

"Hold still a minute." Kam stepped behind me and eased my damp ringlets of hair free of the collar before braiding them into a loose plait down my back. His movements paused. I watched in the mirror as his gaze landed on the back of my neck and stuck. I thought he must be staring at the bruise blooming there. After a moment, he resumed braiding, and my eyes slipped closed as his fingers brushed my skin.

"Food," Jax said. "Then sleep. When you're recovered, we'll worry about the rest of it."

TWENTY-FOUR

Leona

JAX OPENED a connecting door and led us through to a larger room. I stopped dead in my tracks as our surroundings registered. The room was spacious and windowless, softly lit by lamps shaded with Tiffany-style red and orange glass. Hardwood flooring formed a walkway around the perimeter of the room, but the center was sunken, surrounded on two sides by an overstuffed sectional sofa strewn with mountains of soft pillows.

The floor was piled with thick fur rugs. Other odds and ends of furniture occupied the third side of the pit—a comfortable looking recliner, an oversized beanbag, and a low divan in some unusual modern style of design, with exaggerated, ergonomic curves in the seat. Bookshelves lined the far wall, stuffed with mismatched paperbacks of all colors and sizes.

"What on earth?" I asked blankly.

Another door in the room opened and Flynn entered, balancing a tray in one hand. "Much better than that dump in Romania, right?"

"Omega-friendly safehouses are a bit easier to come by when we're closer to our home territory," Jax put in. "But like I said, the serious talk can wait until you're recovered."

Flynn made his way down into the sunken den and set the tray on a corner table by the sectional. "Speaking of which, Beckett and Alex just headed out to meet with someone about… all of this." He gestured around to encompass the entire situation.

Kam straightened at his words, a thread of tension creeping into his bearing. "And once they've had this meeting, Beckett will explain exactly what's going on?"

"Yeah, he will," Flynn said.

"It's a complicated situation," Jax put in. "Especially after the raid last night. But we won't abuse your patience any more than necessary."

Kam sighed. "No. I get it. I'm taking a lot on faith here—but I'm also painfully aware of what the alternative would have been." His deep brown gaze fell on me, and it was haunted.

"Food," Flynn declared, before the creeping sense of disquiet rising inside of me could gain a solid foothold. "No fish meatballs, I promise."

Jax gave him an odd look. "Fish… *meatballs?*"

"Don't ask," Kam told him, giving a delicate shudder of distaste.

In fact, lunch consisted of chicken soup and buttered hunks of French bread, with a glass of sweet tea on the side. I curled up in the corner of the couch with the bowl on my lap and ate it. When I was done, I set the bowl back on the tray. It was sitting next to a discarded book on the little table — *The Unbearable Lightness of Being* by Milan Kundera. The blue cover had a drawing of a man's bowler hat above a woman's bikini, the wearer of the clothing invisible so it appeared to hover in midair.

I'd been meaning to read that one.

"Want seconds?" The question drew my attention back to Flynn.

I shook my head. "No, thank you. That was delicious, though."

It had been, too. Rich and perfectly seasoned. Filling, without being heavy. Comforting, with all the nostalgia of childhood and loving, familial care.

Flynn smiled, the dazzling openness of it lightening the invisible weight on my shoulders. Jax stretched, twisting his left arm and wrist back and forth as though to ease the muscles.

"Right," he said. "Make this place up however you'll be most comfortable and get some rest. Flynn and I will keep watch — not that there's anyone out here to bother us, but still. You don't need to worry about anything. Sleep as long as you like."

"God, that sounds good," Kam said, sounding exhausted. "Thank you both."

The pile of thick fur rugs that covered the floor of the sunken den called to me, even as distracting thoughts pulled at my awareness. Kam, whose mind often ran on parallel tracks to mine, helped me toss pillows into the cozy space. There was a stack of fuzzy blankets lying folded next to the far end of the sectional. He grabbed a couple off the top, and we curled up together in a soft cocoon, with Kam spooning me from behind.

Jax moved around the room, turning off all but a couple of the lamps. He and Flynn settled in comfortably on the couch, where they spoke in soft murmurs about plans for bringing in fresh supplies and acquiring clothing for Kam and me. Before long, it faded into a comforting background noise, weaving seamlessly with the reassuring scent of alphas on guard.

Despite his clear exhaustion, Kam's breathing didn't deepen into the slow rhythm of sleep. I dozed, but something was nagging at my mind in a way that wouldn't allow it to quiet completely.

It was the book. *The Unbearable Lightness of Being.* The title had stared me in the face, clear as day. But... in dreams, I could never read written text. It wiggled around, refusing to settle long enough for my eyes to make sense of it. Newspapers were pure gibberish. Books might as well be written in Sanskrit.

And then there was the chicken soup. Food in my dreams was always tasteless. The soup should have been a chicken-and-noodle shaped void against my taste buds. Instead it had been rich and delicious, subtly different from the way my mother had always made it.

A soul-deep chill crept through me again, spreading from the inside out. The hazy pall of unreality draped across the events of the last twelve hours began to thin. A faint tremor took up residence in my muscles as the slight remove that had separated me from the rest of the world settled back into place.

"Leo?" Kam's arms tightened around me as my breathing grew ragged.

"Oh, god," I whispered. "It's real. It…" My voice caught, and I swallowed. "It all… really happened?"

Kam pressed his lips against the top of my shoulder, his embrace never wavering. "It really happened. I'm so sorry, *odama*."

I shuddered, curling forward around the pain of understanding. Our old life was gone. Every possession I had ever owned — *gone*. My bank accounts would already be locked. I didn't have a single penny to my name. I would never speak to my friends or colleagues again without risking arrest — both mine, and theirs. Any small chance Kam and I might have had at making things better for alphas and omegas through our positions in government — *gone*.

I—who had never known suffering or deprivation for a single day before that fateful morning when we were kidnapped in Romania—did not possess so much as a single item of clothing. And I'd brought Kam down with me, through my own stubbornness and self-absorption.

My entire body shook with the effort to keep from shattering into a million razor-edged shards. I couldn't breathe.

"Alphas?" Kam's voice was soft. "Leo needs you now, but she won't ask. Not for herself."

Fabric rustled, and Flynn lowered himself to sit in front of me. I could hear Jax settling in behind Kam. The scent of woods and spice surrounded us in a comforting cloud.

"Is that right, Leona?" Flynn asked. His big hand eased the blanket back so he could see my face. "Do want us to look after you both for a while?"

This was happening. The alphas were here, and it wasn't a dream. Any decisions I made would have real, actual consequences for our future. And yet... it still didn't matter—because right now, for me, there was no future. Yesterday's world no longer existed; tomorrow was a blank and impenetrable vista.

I couldn't protect Kam.

I couldn't protect myself.

I was powerless to face this future on my own. The awareness of my own utter helplessness slammed into me like a hurtling boulder. I needed their strength because mine was gone, and it wasn't fair to steal any more of Kam's.

"Please, alphas," I managed around a choked sob. "Oh, god. I don't know what to do now. I don't know what to do—"

Flynn settled onto his side, facing me. His thumb swiped over my cheek, wiping away the tear that had fallen. He scooted forward, one strong arm worming its way beneath me until my head was pillowed on his bicep. The other draped over my waist and settled on Kam's hip, pulling us both snug against his body.

We were jostled lightly as another big body lay down behind Kam. Jax's hand settled on my shoulder. Low rumbles vibrated around the nest—a pair of alpha purrs.

"I love you, *odama*," Kam whispered against the bruised skin of my neck. "I know it feels like the world is ending, but I've done this before. I promise you, it's really not."

His lips pressed against my mating gland, and the last shreds of my control cracked. I huddled between the alphas and my *odama*, my entire body shaking with helpless, wracking sobs. All of the mastery I'd deluded myself into believing I held over my own life had been an illusion—and that realization hurt like knives flaying my skin.

The only shelter left to me lay in the small pack of misfits who'd somehow seen fit to save my sorry ass... and my packmate's.

Kam knew this pain intimately--he'd experienced unimaginable horrors as a child. And yet, he'd managed to survive and grow into the beautiful omega I loved. I owed it to him to survive as well.

"Kam," I choked out. "I'm sorry. I'm so sorry. This is all my fault."

Kam only squeezed me tighter.

It was Jax who spoke. "It's the fault of the world we live in. You were trying to change that world. There's no blame in that. And maybe you can still change things... just in a different way."

"*Jax*." There was a hint of chiding in Flynn's tone.

"I know, I know," Jax said. "Anyway, that's for tomorrow. Tonight, it's okay to grieve. God knows, we've all got way too many things to mourn."

My remaining strength dissolved like snow in a warm spring rain. With no barriers left to hide behind, I let the tears come, held close and protected by my pack that might have been.

TWENTY-FIVE

Jax

NO QUESTION about it—these two were going to be our kryptonite. I'd thought as much in the cave in Romania, and seeing Flynn with them had confirmed it. The twisted part of it? In some ways, things had become *less* complicated now that their lives had been thrown into chaos.

Leona McCready would never have voluntarily given up her crusade to effect change from her post inside the Foreign Office. And, in my defense, I'd certainly never wanted to see her in this situation, even though something like this had been more or less inevitable. Her secret was already out. Members of the Beta Liberation Front had discovered her omega status, and we hadn't managed to track them down and silence all of them afterward.

We were always going to end up here, or somewhere very like it.

At least Beckett and Alex had managed to extract her before the worst happened. Meanwhile, Flynn and I had whisked Kam away from his apartment before anyone in the MPD had thought to go snooping around Leona's closest colleagues.

From what I gathered, the terrorists still thought Kam was a beta. Even so, it wouldn't be long before the wrong people started making assumptions, especially once they realized he'd disappeared at the same time she had. At least he hadn't been swept up and charged before we got to him.

"I think she's asleep," Kam said quietly.

Adding omegas into our pack wasn't something I'd ever really aspired to. Or at least, it hadn't been something I'd aspired to until Flynn planted the damned idea in my head—and that had only happened recently. Dangerous for them; dangerous for us. Impractical on all fronts, or so I'd always believed. There was, however, no avoiding the fact that having the two of them tucked between us like this felt right.

"She needs the rest," Flynn said. "So do you."

Kam's chest rose and fell heavily within the circle of my embrace. "Yeah."

We stayed where we were until both of them were out cold with the kind of heavy, boneless lassitude that meant they'd sleep for hours. Leona snored softly, congested after crying her eyes out for everything she'd just lost. When I was absolutely certain that the jostling wouldn't wake them, I met Flynn's eyes and gave my head a tiny jerk toward the sofa.

After a reluctant pause, he nodded and eased himself out of the tangle of limbs while I did the same. We tucked the pair snugly into their nest of pillows and blankets, and then flopped onto the sectional nearby. I shook out my left arm as best I could, trying to ignore the shooting nerve pain. That and the damned headaches were the legacy of my stint as an alpha lab rat. It could be worse, obviously... but I chafed at not being at full strength now that the shit was hitting the fan.

"Beckett had better come back with the answer I want to hear," Flynn grumbled.

"I think he will," I told him. "It only makes sense. These two would be wasted hiding away on some remote island. And they'd probably go crazy there with nothing to do."

Flynn shrugged one hard-muscled shoulder. "Wouldn't mind seeing 'em in swimsuits, though."

I stared at him. "Do you ever *not* think with your dick?" I asked, without any real heat.

He grinned at me, a sharply dangerous slash of white teeth in his dark-skinned face. "Well, I mean—sometimes. But just look at them." His avid gaze fell on the pair, still huddled together in sleep. "You're right, though. They'd hate that, I guess."

I sighed, and let my head fall back to rest on the couch. "This is going to mean complete upheaval, and not just for them."

Flynn gave a low grunt. "Alex is barely keeping her shit together."

Our pack leader's hasty retreat earlier hadn't escaped my notice. "She's got reason," I pointed out.

"'Course she does," Flynn agreed. "But I told her we wouldn't let what happened to Irina happen to them, and I was right, wasn't I?"

"It almost did, though," I murmured.

His voice hardened. "Yeah, but it didn't. And it's not going to."

I let him have the last word on the subject, because there was no point in arguing. Flynn had a black and white view of the world that must make the inside of his mind a very straightforward place to be. We all had our pasts, and we'd all been marked in different ways. Alex had built walls of ice around her heart. I'd rebelled against my upbringing in the breeding pens by soaking up every bit of education and culture I could get my hands on, in an attempt to prove that I was more than a dumb animal with a moderately useful dick attached.

Flynn had handed the reins of his conscience to those he trusted, rather than trying to make complicated decisions in a beta-run world that he didn't fully understand. This was, if I were being honest, the first time I'd seen him acting so rebellious about *anything* in a very long time.

"Her next heat is due in nine days," Flynn said.

And... *yeah*. I wasn't exactly unaware of the fact. I hadn't gone out of my way to mark the calendar date or anything like that, but it wasn't as though I could forget it, either.

"You're going to ask them again," I said, with something like resignation.

"You bet I am," Flynn shot back. "Are you sayin' you're not interested?"

I clenched my jaw. "Of course I'm interested, you ass. They're the most amazing pair of omegas I've ever met. Of *course* I am." A frustrated sigh escaped my control. "But unlike you, I'm not willing to spit in Alex's face. She's our pack leader, and this entire situation is driving a knife through her heart—even if she won't show it openly."

Flynn's heavy brow furrowed, the gears visibly turning behind his eyes. "But... that's an old wound, not a new one. You don't get better by stitching something up while the infection's still inside. You have to open it up. Get some sunlight and air on it so it can heal properly."

Fuck. Why was it that every time I discounted Flynn, he came up with something like that? There was a reason I'd thrown my lot in with the giant asshole in the first place, and this was it.

"I'll talk to her," I said. "Actually, we should both talk to her. We need a pack meeting anyway."

"Yeah, no shit," Flynn agreed. "When they get back, all right?"

"Deal," I told him.

He nodded and left me alone on the couch with my thoughts, in favor of easing back into the omega's nest with them. Leona flopped one uncoordinated arm across his stomach and nuzzled into his shoulder without waking. Inside my chest, something clenched with an almost painful tenderness.

<hr>

Many hours later, the sound of an approaching vehicle tickled the edges of my alpha hearing. Flynn raised his head and met my gaze.

"That's the Jeep," he said. "You go. I'll stay with these two."

Kam drew in a breath and opened his eyes, immediately tensing up. "What's wrong? Is someone here?"

"Just Alex and Beckett," I told him, my body cranking up the reassuring alpha pheromones without any input from my higher brain functions.

What did I say earlier? *Kryptonite.*

"You can go back to sleep if you want," Flynn added. "Jax—bring some food up with you afterward."

"Will do," I agreed. Pausing to collect the Glock I'd stashed next to the couch—just in case—I went to meet the others at the door.

They'd brought groceries. Beckett looked tired and drawn, as well he might after the events of the past day. Alex was inscrutable, though she did lock eyes with me briefly as they entered. I gave her a terse *all-is-well* nod, and she nodded back.

"What's the verdict?" I asked, rather than beating around the bush.

"They're in if they want to be in," Beckett said. "How are they faring?"

"Asleep," I told him. "Flynn's with them. Mr. Patel is holding up well, but Ms. McCready is struggling."

"Not surprising," Beckett said. "No matter how prepared you think you are, when it actually happens, you find out you're really not."

I gave a considering nod. "I'm getting them some food for when they wake up. Later, though, we need to hold a pack meeting if that's okay, boss."

Alex's posture stiffened almost imperceptibly.

Beckett's pale eyes always saw more than they should, but he only nodded. "I can take the food upstairs and relieve Flynn, so you three can have a talk."

"Thanks, boss," I said, heading to the kitchen to put away groceries and make sandwiches.

Beckett joined me there a few minutes later. He'd lost his jacket, rolled his sleeves up to his elbows, and splashed water on his face. I handed him the tray, and he headed upstairs, leaving me alone with Alex.

"Flynn is going to harp on about exactly what you'd expect," I warned her. "But the thing is, I'm not all that sure he's wrong."

"We can't protect them, Jax," she said.

I let out a breath. "Maybe not, *alef*—but we took a pretty good crack at it this morning. Do you really think they'll be *less* safe with an alpha pack around them?"

Of course, she couldn't say no without it being an obvious lie, and Alex hadn't become our leader by lying to us.

"Let's wait for Flynn before we get into it," she said instead.

Our packmate joined us a couple minutes later.

"They're both awake," he said, by way of greeting. "Beckett's gonna talk to them about the offer."

"And you still want to make them a different offer," Alex replied, gesturing the three of us to sit around the battered kitchen table. "You realize their decision on Beckett's proposal will make a big difference here, Flynn. That is, unless you intend to bail on us and run off after them to the South Pacific or something."

"They'll stay," Flynn said with absolute certainty.

"You don't know that," Alex retorted. "They already tried standing and fighting, and look where it got them."

Flynn stared at her. "You have actually *met* Leona McCready, right?"

Alex's lips thinned, and I couldn't get past the haunted look behind her green eyes.

She raised an eyebrow at me. "And where do you stand on this?"

I tapped the tabletop rhythmically with the fingers of my right hand. "The way I see it, there are a couple of options. You and Flynn can throw down, and maybe once you've kicked his ass, he'll reconsider things." Flynn scoffed. I ignored him and continued. "Or we can discuss a compromise."

"I'm listening," she said, not breaking expression.

"Not sure there's much to compromise on," Flynn observed.

"Hear me out," I said. "Leona's heat is coming on in a little over a week. Beckett could probably score a heat blocker for her in that amount of time, but she's already been on that shit for years. Eventually it's going to kill her." This next bit was going to be the tricky part, and I watched Alex's expression carefully. "Or, alternately, he could find her some contraceptives."

Her features froze.

"From a reputable source," I added quickly. "You know Beckett has the right contacts to get the good stuff."

"That's a thought," Flynn said, clearly catching on.

Alex didn't dismiss it out of hand or fly off the handle—and, of course, that was why she led our pack. Well, that and the fact that she could pound both of us into the dirt, if it ever came to that.

"You're talking about a no-strings-attached heat contract. Which, I hasten to point out, is what I thought Irina and I were going to have, before I succumbed to knot-brain in mid-coupling and agreed to give her a mating bite."

"You were alone, and you were both young," I said. "Plus, I hope I don't have to point out that I've been with more omegas than I care to remember, yet I've never been tempted to bite. And Flynn treats sex like it's a recreational sport."

"*Hey*," Flynn protested, sounding mildly insulted. A moment later, he seemed to realize I was on his side in this, and he added, "It's just nice to get close to people, that's all. It doesn't have to be a huge deal."

"We'll all be there to police each other and keep emotions from getting out of hand," I said, hoping to bring my argument home. "This kind of thing wasn't at all unusual in the old days, before the Purge. And isn't that exactly what we're all fighting for? The freedom to be ourselves and manage our lives the way we see fit?"

Alex's jaw tightened, the tendons working with tension for a long moment. "All right." It sounded like the words were being pulled from her. "Counter-proposal. *If* they agree to stay here instead of sneaking out of the country to hide, and *if* they furthermore agree to a heat contract with the two of you—then she uses a cervical cap with spermicide in addition to hormonal contraception, and anyone knotting her wears a condom. I'm present for all of it, and if I see teeth coming anywhere near a mating gland, I will deliver the beat-down of your *fucking life*."

Flynn grinned at her. "Done."

She looked mildly taken aback, either because she'd been geared up for more of a fight, or because she'd just realized that this might really be about to happen. She shot me a sharp look, and I shrugged.

"Works for me," I said, not about to bring up the fact that triple-redundancy in contraception seemed like a bit of overkill, to put it mildly.

She had her reasons. And frankly, I'd expected more resistance, so I wasn't about to make a fuss.

Flynn looked like he could float on air. "Great! It's all settled. Now we just need to wait for Beckett to work his magic."

"Yeah. Great," Alex echoed faintly. "*Fuck*."

TWENTY-SIX

Leona

I WOKE TO the sound of Flynn talking quietly with someone at the door. Kam stirred beside me and sat up, blinking.

My eyes felt gritty; I had the dregs of a crying headache throbbing in my sinuses. I was sure I looked like hell warmed over — puffy and blotchy red. The events of the past day settled over me with cruel clarity, all of the blessed haziness from earlier gone without a trace.

We were fugitives.

We'd lost everything.

It was my fault.

And after all of that, I'd somehow slept for hours in total peace, wrapped in strong arms and curled against my *odama*.

Flynn and Beckett stood together in the doorway, engaged in a low-voiced conversation. Flynn nodded at something Beckett said, and took the plate that the smaller man had been holding. He crossed the room to us and handed it to Kam. It held two sandwiches, bursting with meat and cheese and tomatoes.

"Chief Beckett needs to talk to both of you," Flynn said. "And I need to talk to Alex at some point. If you want me to stay, I'll stay — but you should know that Beckett's all right. You can trust him."

I hesitated. Beckett had saved our lives on at least two occasions… and yet, I still had absolutely no insight into his true motives or goals. Kam and I exchanged a look. He gave a small nod.

"It's fine, Flynn," I said. "Go check in with your *alef*. Thanks for…" The words stumbled to a halt. *Thanks for letting me soak your shirt with tears? Thanks for bringing Kam here so I didn't shatter completely?*

"Staying," Kam finished for me. "Thanks for staying with us, Flynn."

Flynn smiled his big, brilliant, uncomplicated smile. "Any time, ginger tea. Now, listen to what the boss has to say, okay? I'll be back in a bit."

He rose and left with a nod to Beckett as he passed. The security chief had remained at the door rather than barging into the room we were using as a nest. It was an interesting bit of nuance, coming from a beta.

"May I come in?" he asked politely.

Kam roused himself before I managed to. "Yes, of course." He picked up the plate of sandwiches and set it on the corner table. Then he grabbed one of the blankets and draped it over my shoulders, urging me up to sit on the overstuffed sectional. "Please, come in and make yourself comfortable. We do need to have a talk."

I wrapped the blanket around my body, feeling a bit less self-conscious than if I'd tried to face Beckett in nothing but Jax's borrowed T-shirt. Kam waited until the chief had made his way down to the sunken den and taken a seat on the other side of the sectional before settling next to me.

"Thank you," Beckett said.

I took a moment to study him—this mild-mannered, middle-aged beta with the pale, knowing eyes and kindly manner. He looked drawn, with dark circles under his eyes and new lines etched into his pleasant face. I didn't think I'd ever seen him without a suit jacket and tie before—though to be fair, he probably hadn't stormed the cave in Romania while wearing office attire. I'd just been too out of it to notice.

Now, the top button of his shirt was undone. His sleeves were rolled up, baring slender, sinewy forearms.

"It appears we're in your debt, yet again," Kam said. "Thank you for intervening. Though I do have to wonder what consequences you've brought on yourselves by helping us get away."

Beckett gave him a quick, tight smile. "There are times when the consequences of doing nothing outweigh the risks of taking action."

I still couldn't figure out his angle. "Those consequences would have happened to *us*, though. Not to you or your team," I said carefully, hating how the congested quality of my voice declared my earlier tears to the world.

The chief leaned back against the cushions, regarding me. "Ms. McCready. Mr. Patel. What you've achieved in the Foreign Office is extraordinary by any measure. Believe me when I say, the consequences of losing two omegas in positions such as yours would have been enormous."

Kam leaned forward, perching on the edge of the seat cushion. "But we don't hold those positions anymore. Whatever power we might have had before—it's gone now."

Beckett met our eyes, looking from one to the other of us. "You don't hold *those* positions anymore, no."

I stared at him, a crazy suspicion growing. "You and Alex walked into a police station, and walked out with me in your custody. No *way* was that officially sanctioned. There would have been security cameras. A paper trail. You won't have a position left, either."

"Oh, I assure you, I will," he said with a decidedly wry note coloring his voice.

"But not as a federal security agent," I insisted. "So maybe you'd better tell us who you're really working for."

He gave me a satisfied nod, as though my answer had pleased him. "I've no doubt you've both had contact with us in the past—

and in more than one capacity. Unregistered omegas don't rise to public positions without considerable support from behind the scenes."

Kam drew in a sharp breath. "The underground. You're with the *underground*."

Beckett lifted an eyebrow — a tiny flicker of a gesture. "Lost positions or no, the two of you still have contacts in high places, scattered across the world. Some of those contacts will be sympathetic to the alphomic cause. We could use you. Both of you. And — at the risk of being indelicate — under the circumstances, you could use us as well."

I tried not to show outwardly how much I was reeling. "But you're a beta."

That small, secret smile played over his lips again. "You might well think so. And, to be fair, there are many betas in the underground. Not everyone falls prey to the Committee's propaganda machine."

Kam's lips parted. "*Oh*," he said, in the tone of a revelation. "You... you were out sick during the bilateral talks. You were out for a *week*."

"Yes. I'm far too old to rely on blockers for every heat," Beckett said dryly. "Seriously, Ms. McCready — those things will kill you sooner or later."

I caught my breath, realization dawning.

Beckett undid a second button on his shirt and tugged his collar aside, twisting to present his right shoulder to our wide-eyed gazes. A single, perfect bite scar surrounded the place where an omega's mating gland was located — the skin there darkened and raised to indicate that the mating bond had taken.

"Well," I said faintly. "I suppose that explains a number of things."

Kam let out a startled huff, more shock than amusement. "Doesn't it just?"

Beckett's expression turned rueful as he straightened and buttoned his dress shirt. "Indeed. So now, the question once again becomes what you intend to do, going forward. Even in circumstances such as these, with enough lead time, we can still get you out of the country. We could set you up someplace out of the way with new identities. Or... you could join us, with the understanding that you won't be any safer working for the underground than you were while working publicly as unregistered omegas."

My body stilled while my mind processed his words. I stared into Beckett's eyes, searching for any glimmer of insincerity or deceit. I saw only compassion and resolve.

"We'll have to discuss it," I said quickly, even as a faint, burgeoning sense of hope blossomed in my chest.

Maybe this wasn't the end.

I met Kam's soulful brown eyes, and he held my gaze with a look of fond understanding. He'd always wanted a pack — a proper one. And what bigger pack was there than the secret network of alphas, betas, and omegas dedicated to protecting our people from behind the scenes?

"Of course," Beckett said. "Either way, I'm afraid we're going to be stuck here for a couple of weeks at minimum, while more permanent plans can be made. This house is one of hundreds scattered across the country, owned by an utterly unremarkable real estate investment firm with no suspicious ties to anything controversial. We'll stay here and keep our heads down until the scandal of an escaped omega fugitive blows over, and the news outlets start to lose interest."

I couldn't begin to face the reality of my picture being posted all over the front-page news. Not yet. I set that aside for now. There were other things to address, as much as I dreaded doing so.

"I do have another issue," I said.

Kam laid his hand on my blanket-swaddled thigh.

Beckett nodded slowly. "Yes. It's been eleven weeks since Romania. I'm well aware."

I relaxed a bit, still in the process of rearranging my brain around the idea that I was talking to another omega — one quite a bit older than me, who'd had a lifetime of managing heats around the sham of a beta existence.

"It's short notice," Beckett went on, "but barring anything unforeseen, I should be able to acquire whatever drugs are appropriate. However, I'd suggest talking to the alphas first. They're downstairs having a pack meeting as we speak, and you don't have to be a genius to guess what it's about."

I blinked at him. Kam inhaled audibly.

"At any rate," Beckett said, "I should let you eat and talk. There's bottled water in the mini-fridge if you're thirsty. Will you be all right on your own for a bit?"

"Yes," I said, the word so faint it was barely audible. I cleared my throat and added in a stronger tone, "Thank you."

He smiled thinly. "All part of the service. Starting over from nothing is never a pleasant process, but it is survivable."

"And far better than the alternative," Kam replied.

"I've always thought so, yes," Beckett agreed, rising from the couch. "I'll keep the others out of your hair for half an hour, but after that, I'm afraid you're on your own on that front."

With that, he gave us a polite nod and let himself out, closing the door behind him. Silence fell for the space of several breaths, before Kam flopped back against the couch cushions and said, "Holy. Buggering. *Shite.*"

I met his eyes, feeling more than a little breathless. "Do you still want to run?"

He gave a single, high-pitched bark of laughter. "*Odama*, I didn't *want* to run before. I just wanted us both to be safe."

"Staying won't be safe," I pointed out.

He sobered. "No. No, of course it won't be. But Leo—I'm not the one whose door was broken down in the middle of the night. Do *you* want to run?"

I thought about it—about everything that starting over would entail. About the fact that there could well be police or Committee operatives pounding down my door again in the near future. I thought about the underground—the shadowy organization that had saved Kam from slavery and provided me with the tools and contacts necessary to maintain my ruse for all these years.

We could be part of that organization. Next time, *we* could be the people who saved some other terrified omega from a lifetime of horror.

"This morning, I thought it was the end," I said. "I thought it was all over for both of us. But, now? Maybe it doesn't have to be."

Kam smiled at me, gentle and understanding. In perfect synchrony, we fell forward into each other's arms.

"Maybe it doesn't have to be," he agreed.

Beckett was good to his word. Thirty minutes after he'd left us, boots sounded on the stairwell at the end of the hall. A few moments later, the first hints of cypress, jasmine, spice, and musk wafted to us.

I'd eaten my sandwich and had a quick wash in the extravagant bathroom. It had left me feeling marginally more human, at least. A knock sounded at the door, and Kam went to open it, shooting me a speculative glance. I had a fair idea of what to expect after Beckett's not-so-subtle hints, but for now, I knew my answer would have to remain the same.

As much as I might long for it—in the depths of my heart, where I feared to look too closely—there was no way that accepting the suit of an alpha pack during a period of so much upheaval was in any way a sane plan. Flynn would ask us, and Alex would look uncomfortable, and I would politely decline. I would ask Beckett to acquire a heat blocker for me. I'd tackle this new phase in my life with a clear head and no distractions.

Kam would support me—because Kam *always* supported me—and we'd revisit the topic when things were less crazy than they were right now.

"Come in," Kam said, acting as gatekeeper to the nest in the old omega tradition.

"Thank you," Alex replied formally. She led the others into the room, and accepted Kam's offer of a seat on the couch. The others settled nearby, giving us space.

I met her eyes. "Thank *you* for getting me out of that place. I didn't get a chance to say it, earlier."

"That was Beckett's doing, not mine," she demurred. "But I'm relieved we were in time."

The pained look in her eyes made me realize she must be remembering the omega she hadn't been able to save. My heart ached for her.

"Nevertheless," Kam said, taking my hand, "we're immensely grateful to all of you."

"So," Flynn said. "You're both going to stay, right? Join the underground?"

I squeezed Kam's fingers. "Yes. If we can't make a difference from inside the government, we'll try to make a difference from outside it."

Flynn's shoulders relaxed. Alex received the news impassively, but she didn't look surprised.

Jax nodded in clear satisfaction. "I'm glad to hear that," he said.

Kam tilted his head, considering. "Beckett's an omega." His eyes fell on Flynn. "A *mated* omega. You certainly kept that quiet."

Flynn shrugged, completely unrepentant.

"It's not the sort of information one lets slip in casual conversation," Alex observed tartly. "Or in *any* kind of conversation, really."

I thought of the old bite mark, ridged and shadowed in the room's warm light. "It's not… one of you three, is it?" For some reason, I found the idea disconcerting.

Jax let out a startled breath of laughter. "God, no."

"I don't think *anyone* knows who his mate is," Flynn said. "But either way, that kind of information is pretty far above our pay grade."

"I've never even heard him use gendered pronouns," Jax added. "It's always 'they' and 'them.' I'd assumed it was someone high enough up the food chain in the underground that it would be dangerous if the information got out."

Alex shot them a quelling look. "It's not our job to speculate."

"No," Kam agreed. "Sorry—I can see how that would be sensitive information."

"And it's not why we're here, anyway," Flynn said. "We've got a proposal for the two of you."

I steeled myself, sending Kam a mental apology. "I'm sorry, Flynn," I began. "I think I know what you're going to ask, and—"

"No, Leona," Jax said, interrupting. "It's not that. Not what you're thinking."

My jaw snapped shut. After a moment, I regrouped. "Oh? Then, what is it?"

Alex took a deep breath. "Jax and Flynn want to propose a no-strings-attached heat contract. You're due soon, and since we'll be staying here anyway, there's technically no reason why you'd have to use a blocker."

My mind went abruptly, explosively blank. Kam glanced at me, taking in my compete loss of brain-to-mouth functionality.

"A heat contract," he echoed. "You mean in the old sense? A one-time agreement unrelated to courting or mating?"

It occurred to me with a distant sort of recognition that Kam had been born to an ancient, purebred family. They'd followed the traditional alphomic ways, right up to the bitter end. He knew about these concepts as something more than hypothetical. He'd grown up around them.

"That's right," Alex confirmed. "No courting. No biting. Careful and considered use of birth control methods to prevent conception."

"Seriously, you should hear what she's insisting on," Flynn put in. "There won't be a single sperm cell surviving the carnage."

Jax threw him an unimpressed look before turning back to us. His bright blue gaze was serious. "Leona, you don't have to take that poison to stop your heat. Not this time, at least." His expression said *not ever, if we can help it.*

My heart began to pound... with fear, or nervousness, or excitement — I wasn't sure.

Kam's fingers were still tangled with mine, and his grip was almost tight enough to hurt.

"Say yes, Leona," Flynn said. "Kam — say yes."

"You don't have to be alone," Jax added quietly. "Our kind are meant to come together. To help each other."

I tore my eyes away from them — dark and fair, brown-eyed and blue — to meet Alex's gaze.

"You can't be all right with this, surely?" I hadn't meant for it to come out sounding like a question.

Alex drew breath, only to hesitate, choosing her words.

"My packmates don't technically need my permission to offer you a heat contract. It's between them and you." She paused. "And as hard as it is for me to really believe it in my heart, the reality is that it harms no one." Her eyes flickered to Jax for an instant. "Irina and I were young. We were alone. We gambled on black market contraceptives and our own self-control, and we lost. On both counts."

"There will be five of us this time," Jax went on. "All looking out for each other. And, as Flynn says, there will also be more birth control products than you can shake a stick at." His eyes went distant. "There are god-knows-how-many pups with my DNA languishing in the slave plantations. I am extremely cognizant of the dangers involved in bringing new lives into this world."

I swallowed hard, picturing blue-eyed youngsters with chiseled jaws and sandy hair.

I turned to Kam with a pleading look, not sure what I was asking of him.

He gave me a smile, but it was strained around the edges. "I think you should do it, *odama*," he said. "What's the harm?"

But I shook my head. "There's no '*me*' here, Kam. There's only '*us*.'"

"You've got that right, sweet thing," Flynn said. "It's both or neither. Ginger tea, you're gonna say yes and let me see if I can rock your world — beta butchers or no."

Kam froze. "I don't think…"

I caught his gaze, squeezing his hand hard. "We've tried it with bottled alpha pheromones, *odama*," I said. "We haven't tried it with the real thing. Not combined with my heat pheromones."

His lips parted as though he might say something, but no words came out.

"Hmm. That sounded an awful lot like a *yes*, Leona," Flynn said, with a hint of smugness.

I paused, holding my breath.

I could have this.

I could give Kam what he wanted—let the alphas see if they could make him feel good in a way that I couldn't. Not on my own, anyway.

I could experience heat as an omega was meant to, without the worries of public discovery or pregnancy.

We could do this. There was nothing left to stop us. And afterward, we could step away, with no long-term consequences.

"Yes," I said, hardly able to believe it, even as the word left my mouth. "Yes… let's do it. Let's spend my heat here in this house. *Together.*"

End of Book One

The *Secret Pack* trilogy continues in Book Two: *Fight or Fly.*